Curses and Corpses

Witch Haven Cozy Mystery - book 3

K.E. O'Connor

K.E. O'Connor Books

Preface

The Witch Haven series has been created so you spend time with four amazing witches:

Books 1-3 tell Indigo's story: Spells and Spooks, Hexes and Haunts, Curses and Corpses

Books 4-6 tell Luna's story: Muffins and Moonlight, Cupcakes and Cauldrons, Pancakes and Potions

Book 7-9 tell Odessa's story: Hauntings and High Jinx, Hauntings and Havoc, Hauntings and Hoaxes

Book 10-12 tell Storm's story: The Case of the Screaming Skull, The Case of the Poisoned Pumpkin, The Case of the Cursed Candy

And there are two bonus origin stories to enjoy: **Fire Fang** and **Silvaria**

Chapter 1

I paced the wood paneled corridor in the Magic Council office for what felt like the hundredth time. Whenever an employee walked past, I tensed, worried they'd see through my magic disguise and have me arrested.

"Will you stop that?" Olympus Duke muttered. He was lounging in a chair by a set of large sturdy double doors, his eyes half-closed.

I frowned at him. He looked like he didn't have a care in the world and wasn't about to go in front of high up Magic Council employees with me by his side.

Olympus pointed to the chair next to him. I shook my head. He may be able to play it cool, but I was a wanted witch, wearing a complicated magic disguise. And if that disguise broke, I'd be in a whole heap of trouble.

"Indigo, come sit next to me," Olympus snapped. "You're only drawing attention to yourself."

I wiped my sweating palms on the back of my leather pants and perched on the seat next to him. I jumped up a second later. "There's serious power behind those doors. What if someone sees through this magic? They could see who I really am."

"Then we'll both be in trouble if that happens. But it won't. You talk as if you doubt my ability to hold your disguise in place."

I glanced at Olympus. He was tall, dark, and handsome in an uptight way. He was also the Head of the Magic Council, and until recently, had been gunning for me. Now, we were on the same side, but I had no clue how long that would last.

He arched an eyebrow as he caught me studying him. "You doubt me?"

"I doubt everyone, myself most of all." I stared down at my clothing, still not comfortable in my disguise. But this was the only way I could freely move around Witch Haven, without the villagers or the Magic Council pointing the finger and hunting me down.

"We won't be in there for long. They have a fifty point agenda to get through today, so won't have much time to spend on you."

How anyone would willingly work for the Magic Council was beyond me. All those meetings and official rules they needed to abide by would drive me crazy.

"I'll do the talking," Olympus said. "You simply nod and say yes or no at the appropriate time. This is a rubberstamp exercise. They just need to make sure you're fit for duty."

I nodded as I chewed on my bottom lip. I'd give a heck of a lot to have my familiars with me. Nugget would be hanging around my neck and smart talking Olympus, Hilda would be reassuring me as she tap danced on my shoulder with her spidery legs, and Russell would be flying around and making people duck as he dive bombed them.

But I was on my own. In this disguise, no one would figure out I was really Indigo Ash, a failed witch with a murky past. I needed to remain in this disguise until I figured out a way to get my best friend, Luna Brimstone back, then clean up my dubious reputation and that of my stepmom, Magda.

I turned on my heel and almost walked straight into Olympus.

He caught hold of my shoulders. "Take a deep breath and relax. A sweating top lip is attractive on no one, not even you."

I scowled at him and dabbed my top lip. My fingers came away damp. "You'd be anxious too if you were in my position."

He pointed at my mouth. "Keep that shut, nod and smile, and we'll be out of here in no time. Then we can get back to focusing on what's important."

Olympus was right. There were a ton of important things to get done. I had to find Luna, but there was also the not insignificant issue of a dark witch coven infiltrating my wonderful home of Witch Haven. That was also on my list of problems to sort out.

I took in a deep breath and let it out slowly, hoping it would send me to a calmer place.

"That's it. You're doing great."

I nodded and stepped back from Olympus. My opinion of him had changed dramatically over the last week. Initially, I'd hated him. He represented everything I despised. But there was more to him than being an uptight employee of the Magic Council. He had depth, and a tragic past that haunted him. He was also an amazing pancake maker and had a sense of humor, which I was only just discovering.

The more I learned about him, the more I liked. And that was also something to worry about. With so many complicated things to tackle, a tricky romance with the enemy didn't need to go on my list.

The double doors we waited beside were pushed open. "Olympus Duke and Indy Archer." A small, stout elf wearing a stiff collared shirt and green pants looked at us.

"That's us," Olympus said.

"Please, follow me."

"Just remember, play it cool," Olympus muttered as he followed the elf into the chamber.

I cleared my throat and shook out my arms. I could do this. So long as I didn't make any smart comments, we'd be fine. This was going to be a challenge.

I'd been in front of the Magic Council recently, but for a different reason. They'd planned to try me for magic crimes and strip me of my power. But it would be different this time, I hoped. I really hoped it would. I couldn't afford to mess up anymore.

The chamber was full of various members of the Magic Council. They all looked thoroughly bored, and several were asleep.

Presiding over the meeting was a judge I'd met before. Judge Zimmerman was an elderly warlock who radiated power.

He gestured us to a table in the center of the chamber. "Olympus, it's good to see you again. I hear you've been successful in your recruitment of our new ghost hunter."

Olympus inclined his head at me when I lagged behind, so I sped up and plastered a smile on my face.

"That's right. Let me introduce Indy Archer. She came highly recommended and has a knack for communicating with the dead. Given the situation in Witch Haven, she's well-placed to make inroads into the troubles in the village."

Judge Zimmerman peered at me for several long, uncomfortable seconds. "That sounds excellent. And I hear you've already been dealing with a perplexing matter already."

I glanced at Olympus, and he gave me a nod. "You mean Ursa Wyrm?"

"I do. I was speaking to her uncle yesterday. Apparently, Ursa hasn't made a complaint to him in two days. You've done the impossible. You've made her happy."

There were several chuckles from around the chamber.

"I'm glad she was satisfied with my work," I said.

"We are all very satisfied. We're happy to have you join us. May I ask how you dealt with the problems Ursa was having?" Judge Zimmerman said.

I hesitated. Ursa's creepy manor house was far from cleansed of the dark energies and misbehaving spirits that swirled around it. It was hardly a surprise that Gravesend Manor was so troubled, given the place was built on an old graveyard. But I'd found a compromise. A way to keep the troubles and spirits occupied. And that compromise involved the gnomes who lived in Ursa's yard.

Olympus nudged me.

"I communicated with the appropriate energies, and learned of their concerns," I said swiftly. "We came to an arrangement. There may be one or two bumps in the road to iron out, but Ursa shouldn't have any new complaints to bring your way."

"I wish I could believe that. But for now, we're all grateful she's no longer a problem. Long may it last."

There were several muted cheers from around the chamber.

"Indy's work with Ursa was a test of her abilities," Olympus said. "And with your permission, I'd like to make her trial with us permanent."

"I should think so too," Judge Zimmerman said. "With everything that's been going on in Witch Haven, we need all hands on deck. Get right to work, Miss Archer. Welcome to the Magic Council. Olympus will deal with the required paperwork and your salary."

I grinned at him. "Thanks. I look forward to getting my next assignment."

"Very good. You may both leave. Now, let's see what's next on the agenda." Judge Zimmerman leaned over his paperwork.

Olympus gestured me away from the table, and I was happy to hurry out and have the doors shut behind me. It felt like I'd escaped something dangerous.

I breathed out a sigh as we dashed down the stairs and smiled at Olympus. "We did it. We deceived the entire chamber. All those magic users and none of them saw through the disguise."

"You're a genius." He arched an eyebrow. "Anyone would think you have a powerful magic user on your side who created that disguise you wear so well."

I laughed, partly in relief, as we walked along the corridor. I was no longer tense now I'd survived trial by a bunch of bored magic users. "It makes me think the Magic Council isn't that powerful."

"Meaning?"

"Meaning, no one saw through your magic. None of them are that strong. It's all a front to keep other magic users from misbehaving."

Olympus glanced around and then leaned closer. "Don't get too cocky. My magic transformed you, that's why no one saw through the disguise." He wriggled his fingers and magic sparkled in the air. "They wouldn't have just anyone heading up this place. I have serious skills."

"You're very sure of yourself," I said. "No one makes perfect magic."

"I've always been sure of my magic. If you doubt your ability, it'll go wrong." Olympus gave me a meaningful look.

I glanced away. I knew what he was getting at. When I'd arrived back in Witch Haven, I'd had zero belief in myself or my ability to use magic safely. Therefore, what I believed in came true, and every spell I cast had malfunctioned.

I brushed my fingers over the powerful amethyst necklace I wore. Things were changing. And my magic was changing too. So was my belief in myself.

"I have to ask, how did you deal with Ursa's problem?" Olympus said.

We reached the main doors of the building, and a security guard let us out.

"It was easy. I used honey mead."

"You got Ursa drunk?"

I chuckled. "No, but I did a deal with those gnomes who wanted you as their sacrifice. In exchange for a regular supply of honey mead, they're happy to go dark energy hunting. And they love chasing down those evil dolls Ursa insists on keeping. So I arranged for a bunch of merry gnomes to maraud through the place every night and take out the worst of the energies. And it's working. I dropped by to see Ursa just this morning, and she was almost nice to me."

"Wonders will never cease. Ursa Wyrm being a decent witch." Olympus smiled and shook his head. "I'm glad you figured something out."

I stopped walking and turned to face him. "So, now my disguise and my employment as a ghost hunter is official, how about we focus on finding Luna?"

"I have no problem with you doing that. But you also have to look like you're working for the Magic Council."

"And I agreed to do that. I have my disguise on and my magic is primed. I'm just waiting for my next assignment. What will we be doing?"

Olympus worked his jaw from side to side. "We're not doing anything. You'll be working solo."

"Oh, okay. What will you be doing?" It wasn't like I cared. I was used to working alone.

He narrowed his eyes a fraction. "I have business to attend to outside of Witch Haven."

I looked away and frowned. I shouldn't mind that Olympus wouldn't be around. We were still working out what kind of friendship we had. Or even if it was a friendship. Maybe it should be described as more of a twisted business arrangement with a high likelihood of failure and death.

"I won't be gone long," he said. "And as you've pointed out, your magic is firing on all cylinders, so you'll have no concerns about handling a case on your own."

I shook away any thoughts that I'd miss him while he was gone. "You can count on me, boss. But I need to make time to find Luna. It's one of the reasons I agreed to keep this disguise, so I can move around freely and figure out who took her."

"I haven't forgotten. You can work on locating Luna in your free time. But I've already got a new assignment for you, and that needs to be your priority until I get back."

I clasped my hands together. "Please let it be a cute missing magical creature, something fluffy that likes snuggles and doesn't put up a fight when I hunt it. Something that won't blast me to pieces and then eat my bones."

He snorted a laugh. "I doubt these particular creatures will want to eat your bones, but there are no guarantees. I haven't seen them in action."

This didn't sound promising. "What evil critter have you got for me to deal with?"

"I've had a complaint from our Cemetery Guardian, Silvaria Digby. Apparently, the dead are rising."

"Rising as in coming back as ghosts?"

"No, it's more basic than that. Corpses are rising from their coffins and wandering around the cemetery."

"That's... disturbing."

"It is. So far, Silvaria has kept them contained in the cemetery, but the numbers are literally rising. She's unhappy and needs a solution. Your job is to investigate what's making them reanimate and then get them safely back in the ground."

"They're not angry, zombielike corpses, intent on eating my brain, are they?"

"Silvaria made no mention of any attempts at eating brains." Olympus checked his watch. "Go up to the third floor to get the details. There's a file waiting for you."

I glanced back at the building we'd just come out of. "You want me to go back in there alone?"

His smile was sly. "You're a bad, bold witch. I thought you could handle anything."

I grumbled under my breath. "Of course I can."

"Then what are you waiting for?" Olympus said.

"Nothing. I'm just..." secretly afraid of the Magic Council? Wanting to go anywhere but back inside that creepy building on my own? Nervous Olympus will drop my disguise when I'm in a room full of Magic Council employees and leave me to fend for myself because I've annoyed him too many times?

He gave my arm a brief squeeze. "Off you go. I'll be back soon. You can tell me all about the fun you had with the corpses. And keep an eye on Silvaria. She's been working as a cemetery guardian for a long time."

"That's a bad thing?" I'd never met Silvaria Digby.

"Being around dead bodies all the time changes a person."

"Is she dangerous?"

"Anyone with power over the dead is dangerous. Don't expect her to be friendly. She prefers the company of the dead to the living."

"Duly noted. Don't annoy the Cemetery Guardian or she'll set an undead horde on me."

"That's about the size of it. I'll see you soon." He stared at me for a second, then turned and walked away.

I watched Olympus go. He was a strange one, and I had yet to figure him out. He had a foot in two camps. Olympus was committed to the Magic Council, but I sensed an unhappiness in him when it came to his work. He'd also suffered loss and blamed himself for that. There was more to him than just a stuffed shirt Magic Council official. But I needed to make sure I didn't get distracted by poking about in his complex life. I had to focus on finding Luna and clearing my family name. And neither of those things would be easy.

I turned back to the building and reluctantly went inside. I slowed at the end of the corridor by the main staircase as two familiar voices drifted toward me. My eyes widened as Storm Winter and Odessa Grimsbane march past and up the stairs.

I looked around to see if anyone was paying me attention and then followed them. From the angry looks on their faces, they weren't here to make friends.

This day had just gotten a lot more interesting.

Chapter 2

I hurried up the stairs behind Storm and Odessa, drawing close enough so I could hear their conversation.

"We'll make him see us," Odessa said, her usually cheerful face set in a frown. "We've tried being sweet and we've been ignored. And no one ignores my gift hampers. How can anyone be so cold-hearted as to turn down my special pumpkin spiced muffins with the triple chocolate frosting? The man's a monster, and he needs to be stopped."

"We'll stop him. I'm happy to slam my fist in his face until he tells us what happened to Indigo." Storm handled everything bluntly. She was quick with the violence, and her magic always felt sharp and icy.

Odessa was softer and sweeter, but she also came with a dark edge, especially if you got entangled with her enchanted scarecrows. I'd had several meetings with them recently and had the bruises to show for it.

"We'll get him on his own and make him see sense." Odessa marched up the stairs with Storm beside her. "He must realize he's being unreasonable. You can't simply make a person vanish and expect to get away with it."

"Luna vanished," Storm said. "And we still can't get a fix on where she is, or who took her."

"That's different. She was magicked away by a mean ghost with an attitude problem. Judge Zimmerman has to follow the rules. And he's broken them by making Indigo disappear."

I almost stumbled up the stairs. They were here to find out what happened to me? I had to stick around for this, especially if they intended to shake answers out of the judge.

"The Council meeting is in the main chamber," Odessa said as she studied the information board at the top of the stairs. "We'll barge in and insist we're heard."

I opened my mouth to tell them not to do anything risky, but then snapped it shut. I couldn't interfere. They had no clue who I was. If I told them to keep their noses out, there could be trouble. And I'd told Olympus I'd keep my distance from Odessa and Storm. We were close childhood friends, and our magic abilities often combined. If I got too close, they could sense I was wearing a disguise and my cover would be blown.

They were approaching the chamber doors, when two Magic Council guards hurried toward them.

"You were told to wait in reception." A tall guard with a long nose barred them from getting any closer to the doors. "This is a private meeting. It's not open to the public."

I lingered a few feet away, waiting to see what would happen.

"You must be mistaken. We're here for that meeting." Odessa smiled and fluttered her lashes. "Judge Zimmerman is expecting us. I sent him a gift basket with a note to say we needed to meet about an urgent matter."

"You're on the agenda?" the guard said.

"That's right."

Storm stood beside her, glowering at the guards.

"What are your names?" The other guard consulted a clipboard in his hand.

"Let me take a look at that. I'm sure we're on there somewhere," Odessa said.

The guard shook his head and held his clipboard away from her. "I can't do that. Tell me who you are, and I'll see if you're listed. But all the external meeting visitors have already signed in, so you may have missed your slot."

"Judge Zimmerman will make an exception for us," Odessa said. "We're friends. He just loves my pumpkins."

The guard's gaze flitted to Odessa's chest and his cheeks flushed.

Storm scowled at him. "Just check your dumb clipboard."

The guard straightened his shoulders. "Sorry, you're not going in. You need to make an appointment to see the judge some other time."

"This is crucial," Odessa said. "It's a life-or-death situation. Our friend has gone missing, and Judge Zimmerman knows where she is. He took her."

The tall guard frowned. "You're accusing the judge of kidnapping someone?"

"No! I'm sure he'd never do such a terrible thing. But he does know where Indigo is."

"Indigo?" The guards exchanged a glance. "You mean the killer witch, Indigo Ash?"

I grunted softly. It seemed everyone knew my bad reputation around here.

"No, I mean my funny, kind, warm-hearted friend, who wouldn't hurt a fly when she isn't under the influence of dark magic," Odessa said.

I smiled at Odessa's description of me.

The tall guard glanced at his colleague. "If you're friends with that witch, you're not getting anywhere near Judge Zimmerman. You could be dangerous."

"We are dangerous, so you'd better get out of our way." Storm sparked magic on her fingers.

The guards stood firm in front of the doors.

The tall one sighed. "We don't need any trouble. Why don't you ladies go down to the reception area? They've got access to the judge's diary. Maybe they can find you an appointment."

"For today?" Odessa said.

"Doubtful. Maybe in a couple of months' time. He's a busy guy."

"That's not good enough," Odessa said. "Indigo is missing and we demand she's returned to us. We understand she's done a few wrong things and people think she's a bad witch, but she's changed."

I grinned and shook my head as Odessa continued to rant at the stunned looking guards. I had changed since returning to Witch Haven. And I felt like a different person since I'd reunited with my old friends, moved into my family home, and found myself three awesome familiars who stuck by me no matter how many mistakes I made.

"You ladies need to leave," the other guard said. "We're sorry about your missing friend, but this is the wrong place to air your grievance. Go downstairs and fix an appointment to see the judge. Charging in here demanding to go into a closed meeting will get you nowhere."

Storm materialized a long shard of ice in her hand, the length of a javelin. "How about this? Does this get us anywhere?"

Three more guards flashed into view. They all had magic sparking on their fingers, and it was aimed at Storm and Odessa.

My smile slipped and my gut tightened. If they didn't get out of here, they'd be arrested.

Storm turned slowly, eyeing each of the guards like they were something she'd discovered on the sole of her boot. "Five warlocks to handle two witches. You boys must be scared."

"No one is scared, because no one is casting magic in here," the tall guard said. "Everyone calm down. I'll take you downstairs, find you a meeting time, and then you'll leave."

"We're not going anywhere until we see Judge Zimmerman." Odessa stamped her foot, and a curl of orange magic drifted around her.

"Halt from using any more magic." The tall guard was no longer acting like Mr. Nice Guy. His expression was tight, and even from where I stood, I could feel the tension radiating off him. This situation was about to get out of control.

I longed to help Odessa and Storm. If they knew I was standing so close, they'd be fine. But if my disguise was revealed, I'd have no freedom to find Luna or clear my family name.

"This is your last warning," the tall guard said. "Restrain your magic, or you'll be arrested."

One of the guards who'd poofed into existence, blasted a warning spell over their heads, scattering a shower of hot sparks around them.

Odessa squeaked, while Storm scowled at him and lifted her ice javelin.

I turned away. They were powerful witches who knew how to handle themselves. I had to leave them to it. And Odessa was a peacemaker. She'd figure out a solution without them all coming to blows.

"Get off me, you big thug."

I spun back to see Odessa being restrained by a guard.

Storm was sparking ice magic on her fingers and preparing to throw her javelin of ice as two guards advanced on her.

I couldn't walk away from this. There was no way these overly officious guards would arrest my friends for trying to help me.

"Hey, what's going on?" I dashed back, trying to look calm, despite my thudding heart.

One of the guards glanced at me. "What's it to you?"

"I work here. What have these witches done?"

"Interfered with Magic Council business. They're dangerous."

I nodded as I glanced at Storm and Odessa. "It doesn't look like they've done any damage to me."

"Only because we stopped them." The guard looked at me. "Who are you?"

"Indy Archer. Judge Zimmerman just appointed me as a new ghost hunter for the Magic Council."

"I'm happy for you."

I didn't miss his sarcastic tone. "Thanks. I'm thrilled to be here. And I've just taken a huge delivery of cookies to the break room as a sort of getting to know you treat. There is plenty for everyone. But you need to hurry, they won't be around for long. I saw a group of trolls heading that way after I laid them out." I winked at him. "And we all know what trolls are like when they get on the sweet stuff. You think these witches are trouble, trolls on a sugar high are uncontrollable."

Several of the guards turned their heads toward what I assumed was the break room.

"I tell you what, let me deal with these witches. You all look like you could do with a break." I smiled encouragingly at the guards who were facing off with Storm and Odessa. "I'll get them back to reception. I was headed that way anyhow, so it's no bother."

"We are overdue a break." One of the guards nudged his colleague. "And I didn't have a chance for breakfast this morning."

"The cookies are fresh-baked and still warm from the oven. There are even some triple chocolate in there. But remember what I said, the trolls will decimate them if they get first dibs."

The tall guard looked at Storm and Odessa. "No going in the chamber. Stick with this ghost hunter." He looked at me. "If they give you any trouble, you have authorization to use restraint magic."

"Thanks, but I'm sure it won't come to that, will it?" I raised my eyebrows at Storm and Odessa.

Storm scowled at me. But her ice javelin had vanished.

Odessa smiled and nodded. "We don't want to cause trouble. We're just trying to find our friend."

"We'll let these hard-working guards take a break, and I'll see what I can do about your friend." I gestured to the stairs, hoping they'd get the hint and give up the fight.

After a few seconds of hesitation, Odessa walked away.

Storm kept glaring at me. She didn't budge.

I looked at her and shrugged. "You can do what you like, but you're not getting through the magic barrier around the chamber. You need an official invite to get in. Why make this harder than it needs to be?"

"Come on, Storm. We can always ambush the judge when he leaves," Odessa said.

I glanced over to make sure the guards hadn't heard her, but they were already racing away to the break room to grab the imaginary cookies. I wouldn't be popular when they discovered nothing sweet and gooey to enjoy. I could always blame the trolls for eating all the cookies.

Storm gave me a final glare before following Odessa down the stairs.

I hurried after them and over to the reception desk, where there was a queue of people waiting to be seen. "Don't mind those guards. You know what the Magic Council is like. They hate the rules being bent."

"We know exactly how lame and unhelpful the Magic Council is," Storm said. "And since you're a part of this sucky, rule-obsessed place, we don't need your help."

"Maybe we do," Odessa said. "Thanks for the save back there, but I get so angry whenever I think about Indigo going missing. Have you heard anything about her? She came back to Witch Haven recently and got in trouble with the Magic Council. They arrested her, and we can't find out what happened."

"I, um... I'm new here." I couldn't let on everything I knew, but I hated that they were so worried about me.

"You're also useless," Storm muttered. "This is a waste of time. By the time we get in to see Judge Zimmerman, it'll be too late. Indigo will have had her power stripped and be wandering around as a shadow. She'll be no use to anyone."

"Even if that happens, she'll still be our friend." Odessa glanced at me. "Did you say your name was Indy?"

I nodded. "That's right. And you are..."

"Odessa Grimsbane. I live on the pumpkin farm on the edge of the village. I'm also the best scarecrow maker in the magic community. You won't find a better scarecrow anywhere."

"I know. Your scarecrows are awesome."

She tilted her head, a puzzled look on her face. "You've encountered my scarecrows? They didn't do anything bad, did they? They've been boisterous lately."

"Oh, no! I mean, I've seen some scary looking scarecrows about. They must be yours."

"You could be right. Only the most terrifying scarecrows come off my production line. I hand sew the magic into them." She gestured at Storm. "This is Storm Winter. She runs an amazing private detective agency. If you need any underhand business doing, she's your witch."

"I don't do underhand work. Well, not all the time." Storm didn't acknowledge me.

Odessa grinned. "Only about fifty percent of the time."

"It's good to meet you both."

Odessa pursed her lips. "Can you help us get in to see Judge Zimmerman? Are you friendly with him?"

I shook my head. "No, I don't run in the high-up circles. I'm just a lowly ghost hunter. Besides, he won't be useful to you. I doubt he deals directly with lower-level problems like missing witches."

"Indigo is of interest to him." Odessa glanced around. "She got in trouble when she was a teenager. Now she's back, and the Council is interested in her. They think she's dangerous."

I bit my tongue. "What do you think?"

"She's a little dangerous," Storm said.

"Only when she needs to be," Odessa said. "When you get to know her, she's great."

I had to get my friends out of here, but I couldn't risk spending any more time with them, or I'd blow my cover. "Storm's right about this being a waste of your time. I heard the judge is about to leave the village for a couple of weeks, so he won't be around to see you."

Storm turned slowly to face me. "Considering you claim not to know him and you've just started working for the Magic Council, you know a lot."

"Oh, you know, people talk."

She huffed out her disbelief.

"That's unhelpful," Odessa said. "We need to come up with a new plan, but I got so upset thinking about what the Magic Council was doing to Indigo, I didn't think this through." She jabbed a finger into Storm's ribs. "You should have told me not to come here."

Storm choked out a laugh as she rubbed her side. "Why bother? When you dig your heels in about something, there's no point trying to change your mind. You said you wanted to visit Judge Zimmerman, so I agreed." She glanced at me.

I laughed. "That's so true."

They looked at me like I was being weird. I guess I was, since they had no clue who I was.

"Are you suggesting I'm stubborn?" Odessa said.

"I'm not suggesting, you are," Storm said.

"But I'm worried about Indigo. And Olympus Duke has been useless." Odessa went to touch my arm, but I avoided her touch, just in case she saw through my disguise when we made contact.

She gave me another puzzled look. "Do you know him? We keep trying to find out where he's hidden Indigo after he arrested her, but he won't talk."

"I heard Olympus isn't all that chatty," I said.

"He isn't. Although he does have a thing for Indigo, so I hoped he'd go easy on her."

My eyebrows shot up. "Do you really think so?"

Odessa's eyes gleamed. "I do. Come on, you must know something. Have you seen Olympus with a skinny witch wearing grubby clothes and sporting a terrible purple dye job?"

Was she describing me? My clothing wasn't grubby. And sure, I could eat more, but I wasn't that thin. And my hair wasn't terrible, it was just a home done job. "Nope. I know nothing."

"Just like everyone who works here," Storm said. "You'll fit right in."

Odessa sighed. "We need a lead. We can't have more friends vanishing. Losing one is bad luck, but two looks suspicious."

"Let's get out of here," Storm said. "This queue isn't moving."

"Yes, maybe you're right. And I need cookies after Indy told the guards about those triple chocolate cookies she ordered. My stomach is grumbling," Odessa said. "We can grab something to eat and figure out our next move. But I'm not giving up on Indigo. People may think she's a rotten witch through and through, but we know better."

"She is kind of rotten," Storm said.

"Why do you say that?" I asked.

Storm smirked. "You are green if you don't know about the legendary Ash witch."

"Humor me. Why is she so bad?"

"She killed sixty-six people when she was seventeen."

"Not true. She helped her stepmom kill those people. It was a family effort." Odessa turned to me. "Everyone in the village thinks Indigo's a cold-blooded killer, and she let in the darkness that's seeping through this place and turning everyone weird."

"What do you believe?" I held my breath as I waited for her answer. I had no idea this disguise would give me access to the inner workings of Storm and Odessa's minds. I wasn't sure I wanted to know what they really thought of me, but there was no backing out now.

"Indigo is an awesome witch. She'd never ruin Witch Haven. This is her home." Odessa nudged Storm. "Isn't that right?"

"Whatever you say. Let's go grab some cookies."

I hid a smile. That was Storm's way of saying she liked me. My sigh of relief was a little loud, so I covered it with a fake sneeze. "You sound like good friends, looking out for her. I hope you find her."

"We will." Odessa smiled brightly at me. "You know, you kind of remind me of her. I mean, she'd never wear those tight leather pants or that intense eyeliner, but there's something about you..."

I backed away a couple of steps. "I'd better go see if those cookies need topping up."

"Before you do, let me send you a thank you hamper. I do it for everyone who's helpful to me," Odessa said. "Where are you staying?"

"Oh, you don't have to do that," I said. "I wasn't that helpful."

"She really wasn't," Storm said. "Save your treats for someone who deserves them."

"I insist," Odessa said. "And ignore Storm. She gets super mean when she's hungry."

I looked toward the door. I needed to get away before I said too much. "Send it to Olympus Duke's office. He's got a place in the village. Do you know it?"

Odessa's eyes widened. "Oh! You're staying with him? Are you two together? I wondered why you looked so startled when I said he had a thing for Indigo. Don't worry, they haven't done anything. At least, I don't think they have."

My cheeks flushed. "No! It's not like that. He's... he's my boss." And he was, kind of. And we definitely weren't dating, though he had made me breakfast a few times before we started work.

I grimaced. This hiding and disguising business was already getting messy.

Odessa grinned at Storm, who simply shrugged and looked away. "I'll send the hamper there. You and Olympus can enjoy it together."

I continued to back away. "Thanks. That's great. And good luck with finding your missing friend." I turned and hurried away before I put my foot in my mouth anymore. That was way too close, but I was glad I'd been able to stop them getting in trouble. I shouldn't be surprised that they were here hunting for me. They were awesome friends, and I was so glad to have them back in my life.

I dashed to the third floor and grabbed my new assignment. As amazing as Storm and Odessa were, I had to work alone for now, with the occasional help from a gorgeous warlock with an ego.

I shook my head. Olympus and I were complicated, but the mysteries I was struggling to unravel were even trickier. My focus had to be on them, not the tall, dark, and surly warlock who was my new ally.

Chapter 3

"So, where are all you creepy dead dudes hanging out?" I peered through the closed wooden gates of Witch Haven cemetery. It didn't look spooky in the daylight, not with the afternoon sun shining down on the tidy plots and neatly mowed lawn.

I opened the gate and stepped through. As you would expect, it was quiet. And best of all, I didn't spot a single corpse who might shamble over and cause trouble. I eased the gate shut and followed the path around the outside of the grave plots in a large loop.

There were still no corpses rearing up. Had Olympus gotten it wrong? Had the dead just popped out for a stretch and a stroll and were already tucked back in their coffins?

I flipped through the file I'd collected from the Magic Council. There was a short report from Silvaria Digby, stating she'd seen six dead bodies dig their way out of the ground and wander around. They didn't cause any trouble, but they weren't keen on going back in their coffins. A spell of calm had helped keep them in line, and they'd eventually gone back to their eternal rest.

I skimmed through the rest of the notes, but there was nothing useful. Silvaria hadn't sensed any curses or hexes on the skeletons, and there'd been no recent trespassing or malingering energies that could tinker with the dead.

"Maybe you just wanted a fun night out," I muttered as I closed the file and continued my circuit around the cemetery.

Nothing stirred. The dead were still very much... dead.

I looked around some more to see if I could find Silvaria and have a chat with her, but there were no signs of any office or room she might use when she wasn't out tending her dead flock.

After an hour of wandering about, my stomach reminded me I'd forgotten to eat lunch. I left the dead to their slumbering and strolled into the village to see what I could find. It still felt strange to walk around without someone throwing something at my head or casting a spell on me. My ghost hunter disguise was holding, and other than a few curious glances, no one paid me any attention.

I walked into Fandango's bakery, owned by Albert Black, Luna's uncle.

He gave me a friendly nod as he walked over. "Good afternoon. Are you eating in or out?"

"I'll take my order to go," I said. "I'd like one of those spicy gravy vegetable pies and a white chocolate muffin."

"Those are excellent choices, and all made fresh today." Albert was a short, nervy man, who never seemed to stop moving. He bagged the goods and handed them to me. "I've not seen you in Witch Haven before. Are you just visiting?"

"I'm new to the area. I've been hired by the Magic Council as a ghost hunter. I hear the village has had a few problems in that area."

His forehead wrinkled. "I can't say I know much about that. This is a peaceful place. Nothing much happens in Witch Haven, and that's how we like it."

It seemed Albert was still being weird. He'd gone from being devastated when Luna vanished, to almost gleeful when her ghost had appeared and he thought she was dead. Now, he seemed to have forgotten all about that.

I handed over some money. "You've not seen anything weird going on around here?"

"Weird is our every day." He handed me my change with a sunny smile on his face. "What kind of weird are you looking for?"

I leaned closer. "I heard the dead are rising."

Albert roared out a laugh. "I should hope they aren't. We like them safely tucked away in the cemetery. I thought you said you were a ghost hunter, not a zombie hunter?"

"Ghosts can reanimate corpses. I'm still figuring out why the dead are rising."

Albert rubbed his chin. "I guess they can. Well, I'm glad you have a new job, but I have a feeling you'll be bored. Like I said, this is a nice, friendly place. We go about our business and keep our heads down." His smile faltered and his eyes narrowed. "And you'd be advised to do the same thing."

I stepped back. There it was, the darkness that lingered inside Albert. He'd been tainted by whatever was messing with this entire village.

I gave him the warmest smile I could muster. "I'll be sure to do that. And I won't get in your way."

His laugh was overly loud again. "You'd better not. Enjoy your food." He turned to the next customer.

I hurried out of the bakery, clutching the bag. The last time I'd eaten anything from Albert's bakery, I'd passed out and wound up on a witch pyre. Should I risk eating this food? I opened the bag and inhaled the rich gravy aroma and the sweet chocolatey muffin heaven. Albert had no clue who I was, and he wouldn't drug strangers or he'd go out of business. The food also looked delicious. It was worth the risk.

I made a quick detour to grab magic supplies from my room in Olympus' office and then headed back to the cemetery. I might as well do something useful while I was waiting for the dead to shuffle out of their coffins and tell me what they were playing at.

After eating my pie, and happily finding it not drugged, I set out the supplies I needed to cast a spell to see if Luna would appear.

I had a vial of prepared potion that should reveal a person's whereabouts. I'd already tried it several times, with no luck, but it was a solid spell and I was determined to keep trying. One day, it would work and reveal where she was.

I unrolled a small map, cast a locator spell, and waited to see if the magic would find Luna.

It failed. I cast again and ate my muffin while I waited for it to work.

The spell had no effect. My magic just couldn't find Luna.

I settled on the bench, rested my hands on my knees, and closed my eyes. Let's see what summoning Luna would do. The last time I'd tried this, I'd had Storm and Odessa with me. We hadn't meant to summon Luna's spirit, but she'd appeared and shocked us all. At least something claiming to be Luna had appeared. I was far from convinced it was her. I'd know if my best friend was dead.

Luna was out there somewhere, and the magic messing with the village had its evil claws in her. And I had plans to rip out those claws and get her back.

I focused on Luna, capturing her image in my mind and picturing her dark, straight hair, wide mouth and intelligent eyes.

With all distractions shut out, I waited. Magic sometimes worked with a snap of the fingers, but the more complicated spells took time, especially when you were working on your own.

A slight shuffling filtered to my ears.

I tilted my head and opened one eye. A small racoon wandered past. "I don't think I've summoned you with magic."

He wandered off, happy to keep snuffling and snorting as he searched for food.

I closed my eyes and continued to focus on Luna, willing her to reach out and give me some sign she was alive.

Nothing happened.

I let out a slow breath, trying not to feel defeated. Wherever Luna was, she wasn't able to reach out to me.

I packed away my magic equipment and did another circuit of the cemetery. There were still no shuffling skeletons about, so I headed to my temporary accommodation in the back of Olympus' office.

Once I was inside, I locked the door behind me. Olympus had only been gone a day, and I was annoyed with myself for missing him. We didn't have that kind of friendship. I was only missing him because he'd forbidden me from seeing my friends and was keeping me away from my familiars.

I put away my magic equipment and wandered around the office. What was I supposed to do? I couldn't find Luna, and there were no corpses to chase. I turned to the pile of folders on Olympus' desk. Maybe there was something interesting to read inside them.

My gaze shifted to the toy leopard on the edge of the desk. "You're new." I walked over and picked him up. He was plump and soft and had a goofy smile on his face. "I can't imagine Olympus buying you. Were you a gift?"

Unsurprisingly, the toy leopard didn't answer.

I set him back on the desk and gave him a quick pat on the head. "Olympus won't mind if I take a look through these files. If he didn't want me looking at them, he wouldn't leave them out. Am I right?"

The leopard said nothing.

I perched on the edge of the desk and picked up the first file. I was flicking through the top pages, when there was a soft thump behind me.

I turned to see the leopard was gone.

"Sorry, buddy. I must have bumped you with my hip." I hopped off the desk and went to retrieve him. There was no sign of the stuffed toy.

I got on my hands and knees and looked under the desk. He wasn't there. When I stood, he was back on the desk.

I narrowed my eyes. "I don't think you're an average toy, are you? Come on, reveal yourself. What exactly are you?"

It didn't move.

"If you don't show me what you are, you'll get no more head pats."

The air heated around me, and I took a step back, not taking my eyes off the toy. There was a blast of red light, and as I blinked the dazzle out of my eyes, an enormous, life-sized leopard stood in the office. It shook out its fur and did a long, all over body stretch.

I backed away to the door, magic primed on my fingers, just in case this leopard wasn't friendly.

It yawned, exposing a magnificent set of sharp teeth, and huge amber eyes blinked at me.

"Um... hi. Do you talk? Or do you attack first and ask questions later?" I said.

The leopard wagged its tail. I thought only dogs did that.

It opened its mouth as if to roar, but instead, a squeak came out.

The leopard twitched its whiskers and tried again. This time, the roar was only slightly more impressive. It gave a hacking sound and shook out its fur again, then lay on the floor and rolled onto its back. I didn't need to look hard to see this leopard was all male.

"Hey, buddy. Are you friendly?" I took a step closer.

The leopard looked at me and waved his legs in the air.

"You're asking for a belly rub?"

The tail wagged wildly.

"If you bite off my arm, you're in serious trouble." I inched closer, knelt, and stretched out my hand, before giving his belly a quick scratch.

A deep, floor trembling purr rolled out of the leopard. His eyes rolled back in his head and his tongue fell out.

"I've found your weak spot." I kept scratching, growing in confidence when the giant cat made no attempt to eat me.

A spark of magic shot out of my hand and hit him in the belly. I whipped my hand back. "I'm sorry. I didn't mean for that to happen. My magic can be a bit off at times. These powers are new to me."

The leopard blinked at me. "No apology needed. And that wasn't you, that was me. I needed an energy boost so I could find my voice."

My mouth opened, but nothing came out for a few seconds. This leopard had the most adorable high-pitched voice I'd ever heard. When you imagine a leopard talking, and I do that all the time, you'd expect him to be deep and growly. This gorgeous guy sounded like he'd sucked on a helium balloon.

"More belly rubs?" he asked.

"I, um, sure. I'm Indy. Who are you?"

"You're not Indy. I know who you are. I've been in this office this whole time. I've heard everything."

"You have? Where have you been hiding?"

"In that cupboard in the corner. Olympus put me in there after... well, I don't like to talk about it. I'm Monty. I'm Olympus' familiar."

My eyebrows shot up. "He's never mentioned you before."

The goofy smile on Monty's face vanished, and his big furry nose wrinkled. "We've had a few issues. Our relationship is complicated."

I continued stroking my fingers through his thick belly fur. Power radiated out of this familiar like sunrays. I shouldn't be surprised he was connected to Olympus, given how powerful he felt.

"So, you know everything about me?" I said.

His amber eyes gleamed. "I know all about you, Indigo Ash. And I'm excited to meet Nugget. I'm so jealous you let your cat familiar join you on your adventures. Olympus never takes me anywhere."

"You must have done something really bad if he turned you into a toy and stuck you in a cupboard. I can feel your power. Olympus is at a disadvantage by not having you at his side."

"As I always tell him. You give great belly rubs. More, please."

I settled on the floor beside the cat and got down to some serious belly tickling.

He rumbled more floor shaking purrs as he waggled his feet in the air. Maybe Olympus was hiding Monty because he didn't add to his alpha male reputation. Monty was just a big, lovable fluff ball.

"Monty, don't take this the wrong way, but you're not how I imagined Olympus' familiar. I mean, you look the part, but..." how could I say anything about his goofy personality without offending him?

Monty kicked his legs in the air. "I'm just what he needs. And I compliment him. Familiars take on some of their magic user's characteristics. We blend with each other."

A burst of laughter shot out of me. "You're telling me Olympus wants his belly rubbed?"

Monty chuffed out a laugh. "Just like me, he wants to be loved. And you must have noticed your familiars have the same characteristics as you. Do you really have three?"

I nodded. If that was true, that made me snarky, greedy, and sometimes mean. But it also made me wise, brave, and inspiring. That was a lot to take on board.

"Do you know when Olympus is coming back?" I said.

"Not until tomorrow," Monty said. "And you need to convince him I can stay in this form. I don't like being transformed. And I'll promise him I won't embarrass him ever again."

I couldn't wait to hear the story behind this. "I'll do my best. And while Olympus isn't here, he can't stop us working together. How would you like to go on an adventure?" Since I was lacking inspiration about how to find Luna, and getting nowhere with my corpses, I had another mystery that needed solving.

Monty jumped up and did zoomies around the room, almost knocking me over as he flew past. "An adventure! Where are we going? What are we doing? Do I have to eat anybody?" His fur bristled out all over his body.

"Calm down! This mission calls for discretion. And since you know everything that's been going on, you know how important that is."

Monty lowered to the floor. "I can do discreet. I do the best belly sneaking move you'll ever see. Watch." He scuffled around on the floor, his head darting from side to side as if he was looking for something to catch.

"That's impressive. But you need to be discreet and quiet. Are you up for the challenge?"

He stood and waggled his ears at me. "Always."

I grinned at him. Hanging out with Monty could be fun. "Great. Let's go break into a house."

Chapter 4

"Are you sure you know what to do?" I said to Monty.

He stood beside me as we lurked by a large oak tree. "I'm the diversion. If we get spotted, I make a noise and then go on the attack."

"No! No attacking. No one gets injured on this mission." I'd waited until dark before leaving Olympus' office with Monty and walking to my family home. This was where I'd grown up with my dad and my amazing stepmom, Magda. After they died, I inherited the house, but it came with a lot of strings, and I was still untangling them. The house was also where I'd find Magda's journals, and I needed those. I'd already found one message in a journal that revealed Magda was blackmailed by a dark witch coven to do their bidding. I was hoping I'd find more information about this coven in the journals. But first, I needed to get my hands on them.

And since, technically, I was missing, I couldn't stroll into the house and take what I wanted. That was why I was doing a little discreet break and enter with Monty as my backup.

"I'm guessing Nugget, Hilda, and Russell will be at home," I said. "They're protective of this house. They'll defend it when they see you."

"I understand. I'm also protective of wherever Olympus lives."

I tilted my head. "Other than the office, where does he live?"

"He moves around a lot. He used to have a place here with Peony and Bloom, but you know what happened there. After Bloom went missing and Peony left, he became a bit of a drifter. I keep telling him to find a place with a huge yard for me, but he won't listen."

I nodded. Olympus had once been engaged to Peony Cashmere, but they'd separated after their daughter had vanished.

"You sneak around the front and make some noise. That should get everyone out of the house. While they're investigating what's going on, I'll sneak in the back, grab the journals, and we'll meet back here. Got it?"

"Got it. I eat the bird, squash the spider, and—"

"No! Monty, no killing my familiars. Unless you want to be turned back into a soft toy, you'll do as I tell you."

He chuffed out a laugh. "I'm only teasing."

I didn't know him well enough to figure out if that was true. "If you get the urge to eat or squash anything, then run in the opposite direction. I'd rather this mission failed than I lose my familiars."

His tail lowered. "Leopard's honor. I won't let you down."

I bit my bottom lip. It wasn't too late to turn back, but I did want to look at those journals. There had to be more information in them about the coven messing with Witch Haven.

With a nod at Monty, I ducked behind the tree and watched him lope to the front of the house. After a few seconds of silence, he started crashing around and making a ridiculous amount of noise. Perhaps I should have told him to be a little more discreet.

I followed him a short way until I could see the front door. It didn't take long before it slammed open. Russell burst out, cawing and circling around. Nugget wasn't far behind, with Hilda riding on his back.

That was perfect. With all three of them out the front, I could get what I needed, and they wouldn't know I'd snuck in.

I dashed around the back of the house and tried the door. It wasn't locked. I eased it open and hurried through the kitchen. I took a second to breathe in the familiar smells of home, then raced into the living room. Magda kept her journals in the magic cabinet in one corner.

I pulled open the bottom drawer and instantly got a hit of lemon wax. It always smelled so sweet, it was as if the magic cabinet cleaned itself.

Inside, there were fifteen journals, all full of Magda's scribblings.

I loaded them into the bag I'd brought with me, but had to carry the last few because I had no more room.

There was a loud thud from outside and a high-pitched squeak that sounded like it came from Monty.

I glanced out the window and gasped. Monty was curled in a ball, his body quivering. Russell was flapping over him. I couldn't see Nugget, but Hilda stood in front of Monty, tapping her front legs on his paw.

I groaned. Please don't tell me Monty was afraid of spiders? Look at the size of him compared to her. How could he be scared of such a small creature?

I swiftly closed the magic cabinet and headed back through the house. I got out the back door and paused. I couldn't leave Monty to be attacked. My familiars had power, with Hilda being the most powerful. For such a small spider, what she blasted out of her fangs was scarily impressive.

I dashed back to the trees, tucked away the journals, and then dodged back around the side of the house.

Monty was still cornered by Hilda, and his whimpering sounded snotty, as if he was crying.

I blasted out a fireball which set light to a bush behind them.

Monty squeaked again and rolled over. Hilda dashed toward the fire, while Russell circled the burning bush.

I gestured Monty toward me.

He raced away, his tail between his legs, and we ran to the trees.

I gasped in a breath as we ducked down, and I grabbed up the journals. "What went wrong back there?"

"Hilda's terrifying." Monty's voice quivered. "She's so mean. And she has all those hairs on her body. She started waggling her legs and rubbing her fangs together, and I almost fainted."

"You could have told me you had a fear of spiders."

"I didn't know I was scared of them until I met her. She's an incredible familiar. You're so lucky to have her."

I grinned as we raced away. "And I know it. They're all great."

"I'm not so sure about Nugget anymore. He was rude to me. He said some naughty words. Did you teach him those?"

"No, his rudeness is self-taught," I said. "But I got what I needed, and no one got hurt, so it was a success."

"I don't know about that. I've experienced severe mental distress," Monty said. "I'll need several hours of belly rubs to get over this trauma."

"You got it." I glanced over my shoulder. I hated hiding from my familiars, but this was for the best. If they didn't know I was here, they couldn't get involved, and then they couldn't get hurt. And once all of this was over, I'd make it up to them. Because, as Monty said, they were incredible familiars.

⁂

I rolled over and stretched, before yawning and blinking myself awake.

My eyes focused, and I saw a pair of legs in front of me. I tensed, and shot upright to find Olympus was looming over my bed.

"I, um, good morning?" I looked around, my brain still operating on sleep mode. "You're back?"

"I am. And I should have known not to leave you on your own." His arms were crossed over his chest and there was a familiar scowl on his face.

I gestured for him to turn around, then grabbed my clothes and pulled them on, before smoothing down my bed hair. "What do you think I've done?"

"I don't think anything, I know all. I've been talking to Monty."

"Your familiar is great. Why have you been hiding him?"

He glanced at me to check I was fully clothed, then turned back around. "I'm more interested in how you managed to reanimate him. That spell should have been unbreakable."

"I'm not sure I did. I mean, I just found him sitting on your desk. I gave him a stroke, and then he started moving around. The next thing, there was a blast of light and Monty appeared. Maybe he did it to himself." I walked to the door. "Is there coffee?"

"There could be." Olympus' scowl remained as he followed me out of the room. "You must have been the one to change his form. Monty couldn't have broken that spell on his own."

I turned to him. "I don't know what to say. It happened. And I'm glad it did. That's not a nice thing to do to your familiar. You owe him some serious belly rubs."

Olympus groaned. "Please don't tell me you've been indulging him. He's impossible once he thinks he's got someone to scratch his stomach."

"He's adorable. You should be proud of him."

"I should. But after everything he's done to me…"

I grinned. "Go on. He said something had happened between you two."

"Let's leave that for another time. You've still got more explaining to do."

I tipped my head back. "You shouldn't interrogate someone before they've had at least one mug of coffee. What do I need to explain?"

"You need to tell me why there are three dead bodies in the office."

My mouth dropped open. "Dead bodies?"

"Follow me."

I stumbled after Olympus and into the office.

Monty bounced to his feet and wagged his tail. "Morning, Indigo. We've got guests."

"Hey, Monty." I scratched his head, but my attention was on the three animated corpses sitting in the visitors' chairs. "Huh! They weren't there when I went to bed last night."

"They arrived not long after we went to sleep," Monty said. "They tapped on the door, so I let them in. I've been guarding them to make sure they didn't eat you in the night."

I stared at the corpses. They stared back. Well, the ones with eyes did. "They wanted to eat me?"

"Isn't that what all zombies want to do? They're not talkative, but they shambled around for a bit and kept trying to get into your room. I had to get snappy with one and give him a nip. In the end,

I guided them to these chairs, and they seemed content to wait."

"What are you doing bringing the walking dead in here?" Olympus said to me.

"I... I didn't bring them here. At least, not intentionally. Maybe they followed me from the cemetery. I went there after I got my assignment and had a look around. There was nothing stirring, and I didn't see a single corpse. I couldn't even find Silvaria to talk to and find out more about why the dead are rising."

Olympus scowled at me. "Did you do anything in the cemetery that would have alerted them you were there?"

I winced. I had cast a lot of magic while I'd been killing time. "I ate a pie. And a muffin."

"What flavor was the pie?" Monty said. "I like chicken. I like all meats. Actually, I need breakfast. Olympus, can we eat?"

Olympus continued to glare at me. "Indigo, what did you do?"

"Nothing bad. I went to the cemetery, looked around, found nothing, so got some food and picked up some spell casting bits and bobs."

"Bits and bobs? Did you cast magic in the cemetery?"

"Yes, but nothing to do with raising the dead. I was trying to find Luna."

He rubbed his forehead. "The last time you did that, she returned as a ghost."

"An alleged ghost, and that was only allegedly Luna. She's still alive."

"Even so, wherever she is, she could be stuck between worlds. You summoning your missing friend in the cemetery aggravated these corpses. They've attached themselves to you."

I glanced at our ripe-smelling guests. "They don't seem that attached to me. I'll take them back to the cemetery as soon as I've had my coffee."

Olympus heaved out a sigh. "Why did I think leaving was a good idea? I'm gone for one day and you've lost focus on your mission. And you've made inappropriate friends."

"I lost focus on nothing. And these aren't friends, they're more passing acquaintances." I walked over to the corpses, two male and one female. "Hey, there. Have you got names?"

They all looked at me.

"You're not feeling chatty today?"

They kept on staring. It was giving me the creeps. "Is it my fault you're here? Did you see what I was doing in the cemetery?"

No one replied to my question.

"Did you really look for any corpses when you were in the cemetery? Or did you spend all your time casting magic to find Luna?" Olympus said.

"I had a job to do, so I did it. I spent ages poking around, trying to get a corpse to bite, but everyone was asleep. Maybe the dead rising was a one-off thing."

"No, Silvaria recorded three incidents of wandering corpses over a single day. If you'd read the file—"

"I did! It wasn't all that interesting. Does Silvaria have any idea why they're wandering about?"

"She doesn't. That's why she asked for our assistance." Olympus studied the corpses for a moment. "Monty, keep an eye on them. Let me know if they make a move."

"Yes, boss. I won't leave my post for a second." Monty wagged his tail, then growled at the corpses.

I lifted my nose and sniffed the air. Under the mildly unpleasant odor of corpse, I got a whiff of something else. Something much more delicious. "Did you bring breakfast with you?"

A smile shifted across Olympus' face. "I might have done. You can catch me up on all your adventures while we eat."

I grinned at Monty and gave him a thumbs up, before hurrying after Olympus.

He opened a bag on the counter of the small kitchenette and pulled out donuts and two takeout coffees.

"You sure know the way to a girl's heart," I said.

He glanced at me. "Is that so?"

I grabbed a donut and stuffed it into my mouth, before I made any more stupid comments. "This is good. Thanks," I mumbled.

"My pleasure." Olympus turned, took the lid off his coffee, and took a sip. "So, don't leave anything out. What have I missed?"

"You're up to speed on the corpses. The cemetery was quiet. There's nothing to work with."

"And what else?"

I ate more donut. "Nothing else springs to mind."

"I'll remind you that I have been talking to Monty. He has a tendency to overshare."

"Oh! Do you mean our little trip to Magda's house? That was nothing."

"That's a different story to the one I heard. The way Monty told it, there was an enormous spider about to savage him."

"Monty was talking about Hilda. And you've met her. She's the sweetest spider around."

"He said she was enormous. Did you cast your magic on her? Do your familiars know you're still here?"

"I didn't touch them. I stayed out of the way. Monty was my distraction, so I could get into the house—"

"You went inside that house? Are you out of your mind? Your familiars could have seen you."

"But they didn't. Monty was great and kept them distracted out the front while I ran in, grabbed Magda's journals, and left. I figured I might as well do something useful while I don't have a job to do."

"You do have a job. You should have stayed in the cemetery until nightfall. That's when the corpses are the most active."

"I didn't know that. I didn't see that information in the report."

"That's because you didn't read it properly."

I resisted the temptation to argue. "I'll go back tonight. I need to return those guys out there, anyway. But I got the journals. That's good news."

Olympus passed me another donut. "Have you found something interesting in them?"

"All of them are interesting. It'll take me time to read through them, but these could be what we need to help get rid of the darkness troubling Witch

Haven. Magda could have left more clues for me to find."

He grunted, not seeming impressed by my efforts.

"And if that darkness is connected to Bloom going missing, it could help get her back, too."

Olympus tensed for a second before he nodded and drank more coffee. "If this witch coven took her, I hate to think what they've been doing to her. She's such a sweet child."

"If they've hurt her, you'll make them pay. But focus on getting her back first. Magda was clever, and she missed nothing that went on in Witch Haven. She could have information to help us."

"She missed the darkness that crept in and got both of you."

I scowled at him. Despite the caffeine hit, Olympus was still grumpy. "Apart from that. And everyone missed that, including you and the entire Magic Council, and you're supposed to be the experts around here."

He didn't say anything.

"If there's anything in the journals that'll help us, we can find it and put a stop to this dark magic."

"You're taking too many risks," Olympus said.

"That's not true. I've taken a few very small risks in the last twenty-four hours."

"And you're still keeping things from me. I know about the fight at the Magic Council. That's not a small risk."

I grimaced. "How do you know about that?"

"I get reports about everything."

"It was a misunderstanding that quickly got sorted."

"And you talked to Storm and Odessa, despite me telling you not to."

Jeez! This guy had spies everywhere. "They were defending me, and at risk of getting arrested. If they're behind bars, they can't help search for Luna."

Olympus pressed his lips together, then sighed. "I was gone for a day. Imagine what would happen if I left for a week."

Monty bounded in, his fur fluffed up and his eyes shining with excitement.

"What is it?" Olympus said. "Are the corpses stirring?"

"They're asleep. Or dead. I'm not sure. Either way, they're doing nothing. I got bored out there on my own. And I need feeding."

"Get back out there and make sure they continue to do nothing," Olympus said.

"I also need a belly rub." Monty looked at me.

"Out!" Olympus said. "You're working."

"Just a small one. Your girlfriend is amazing at giving belly rubs."

Olympus sighed again. "Monty, you're on duty. Those corpses are a risk to my safety and Indigo's. Make sure they don't move."

"He can stay for one belly rub," I said. "Those skeletons aren't exactly fast moving, and we'd smell them before we see them."

Monty's tongue flopped out from between his teeth.

"Don't encourage him," Olympus said. He pointed at Monty. "Back on guard duty, or I'll turn you into a toy."

Monty whimpered, before skulking out with his tail down.

"He's adorable. You should be nicer to him."

"If I did that, I'd have familiars like yours."

"Amazingly protective, never let me down, and help me when I really need it? How would you cope?"

"They take liberties, they run rings around you, and they act like they own that house."

"They have lived in it longer than me," I said. "I guess it is part theirs. Maybe I should put their names on the deed."

"Don't. It'll only make it worse."

"Our familiars are here to help us. They're not our servants, as Nugget will be quick to tell you. And Monty is a good leopard. You should give him a break."

"He gets plenty of breaks. And Monty is a menace. Don't be fooled by all that adorable fluff. Now, let's get to work."

"Yes. I should focus on finding Luna," I said.

"No, you need to focus on the corpses." Olympus settled in a chair and ate a donut.

"I've been there and done that. The only ones I found are the ones that followed me home. If that's all I have to deal with, then this will be an easy job."

"Nothing is easy around this place. Take another day to investigate the corpse problem. If you don't find anything after a thorough search of the area, I'll let Silvaria know what happened and mark the case as closed."

"Then I can focus on Luna?"

Olympus nodded. "You can. But there'll be more cases coming your way soon. Being an employee of the Magic Council isn't an easy ride."

"And I'll handle them," I said. "Just as long as they don't get in the way of me helping Luna."

"I'm sure you won't let that happen."

Monty bounded back into the room.

"If I have to tell you one more time—"

"This is important." He slapped a large paw over Olympus' mouth.

"Is it the corpses?" I said.

"No, but there are two witches, some huge scarecrows, and your familiars outside. They're trying to break in."

Chapter 5

I shoved down the last of my donut and raced after Monty into the front office. Sure enough, Odessa, Storm, three mean looking scarecrows, and my familiars stood outside. And they looked scarily determined.

The building shook, and I grabbed the desk.

Olympus was scowling as he raced out to join me. He looked out the window. "Did your friends just do that to my office?"

"Um, maybe. But I don't think they meant to make the walls shake."

"A spell of that magnitude is always intentional. What are they playing at?"

We both grabbed the desk as the building was rocked again by another blast of magic from outside.

"What do we do? What do we do?" Monty zoomed around the room. "Should I go and eat them? That's a lot of witch to eat in one sitting. What about that terrifying spider? And how do you eat a scarecrow? I'm purebred carnivore. Straw won't digest!"

"Monty! Don't eat my friends. I think they're here because of me. They're worried because I've gone missing."

He slowed his frantic zoomies. "So... no witch for breakfast?"

"No! Olympus, you have to give them a more convincing story about what you've done with me."

"I don't. And it's none of their business. The Magic Council was within its rights to have you arrested and taken away. Once you're in the system, there's nothing your friends or familiars can do about it."

"So tell them I've been sent somewhere. Somewhere they can't get to. If you don't, they'll keep knocking on these walls until they break through. And you won't like confronting any of them when they're in a bad mood."

The front door shuddered, as if something hard had slammed against it.

I peeked out to see the scarecrows backing up, about to begin another charge. "We don't have much time. Those scarecrows don't stop moving until they've been pulled apart. Even then, they try to get up."

"Then help me to keep them out." Olympus sparked magic on his fingers.

"What are you planning to do? Don't hurt them."

"I don't need to hurt them. I just need to keep them out long enough so you can leave by the back door. Their magic will soon wear down, and they'll have to leave to recharge. But before you go, I need your help to strengthen this magic barrier."

"I'm not running away from my friends." I'd done that before, and it ended badly.

"I'm not telling you to run. Just hide."

I crossed my arms over my chest. "No! No more hiding."

"Then help me! Strengthen this spell to stop them getting through. If we combine our magic, it should be enough."

I still didn't join Olympus. "These are my friends. I can't use magic against them."

"Indigo! Get your butt over here and help me strengthen the magic barrier." Olympus had his hands held out, a stream of magic blasting against the wall and front door.

I shook my head. Girlfriends and familiars before guys. Always. "We should let them in and tell them the truth."

"The more people who know about your disguise, the more likely your cover will be blown," Olympus said. "We keep this between the two of us."

"And me," Monty said. "I'm great at counting, and that makes three of us who know you're not really you. Oh! Should we include our smelly new friends? If so, that makes... some more people. Well, bodies. Yes, lots of bodies know about your disguise. Is that bad?"

"You don't count, Monty," Olympus said.

"Monty counts." I petted his big, furry head. "And it's not as if Storm and Odessa will gossip about my disguise with anyone. They know the villagers hate me and the Magic Council want me arrested. They'll keep this quiet."

"It's still too risky," Olympus said. "The more variables that are involved, the more likely the risk will grow and this will fail."

The building shuddered again.

I walked over to him. "Do you spend all day running risk assessments through your head?"

"Usually. And it keeps me alive. You should try it, then there might be fewer people wanting you dead."

"I don't want you dead," Monty whispered.

"Thanks, Monty."

"We have to do something to get them out of here," Olympus said. "They're drawing attention to you. People will want to know why they're trying to smash open this building."

There was another thud against the door, and the hinges groaned.

"Those scarecrows are unbelievably strong," Olympus grunted, his forehead beading with sweat as he poured more magic into the barrier.

As suddenly as the magic blasts began, they stopped, although Olympus kept his magic flowing out of him.

"Let me see if they've gone," I said.

"Stay away from the window. This could be a trick."

"My friends aren't devious." They totally were. If they could find a way in, they'd use it. I looked outside to see what their next move would be, but the street was empty.

"What do you see?" Olympus lowered his magic and pulled it back into his hands.

"Nothing. They've vanished." I turned as a grating noise reached my ears. I looked around, but couldn't find the source of the noise.

Olympus tensed and his forehead furrowed. "Now what?"

"It sounds like it's coming from under our feet. Olympus, are there tunnels under this building?"

"Not that I know of."

I poked my head into the next room and squeaked as a large pumpkin rolled toward me. It settled in front of my feet and grinned. A second later, a huge straw-filled body raced toward me. It grabbed the pumpkin and slammed it onto its neck.

I glanced behind the intimidating scarecrow to see a chest of drawers had been shoved to one side, and there was an open grate underneath it.

"Olympus! We have a problem." I dodged out of the way as the scarecrow ran at me. He charged past and raced into the other room. "Look out! You have an inbound scarecrow heading your way." I raced after the scarecrow.

It didn't slow as it barreled into Olympus and slammed him to the floor.

They rolled around for a few seconds, Olympus blasting out magic and cursing as the scarecrow wrapped its huge hands around his throat.

Monty whirled around, snarled, and leaped on the back of the scarecrow. Everything was a blur of claws, teeth, and snarls as straw flew everywhere. Then chunks of pumpkin sailed through the air.

It took Monty less than a minute to rip the scarecrow apart. With a triumphant growl, he tossed away the last of the pumpkin head, flopped down on top of Olympus, and licked his face.

"Urgh! Get off me, you giant furball," Olympus said.

Monty kept on licking and purring.

Olympus tussled with the big cat for a moment, before laughing. He wrapped his arms around the enormous animal and rolled him off his stomach. He gave the cat's belly a rub. "Good work, Monty."

I stared down at Olympus. He was covered in straw, bits of gooey pumpkin, and had several large gashes on his face. "That scarecrow wasn't playing around. It wanted you dead."

"My bruised throat agrees. Odessa needs to keep better control of those things." Olympus accepted my outstretched hand and pulled himself to his feet.

"It's not her fault. Much like the rest of the village, they've been misbehaving."

"Then she needs to stop making them until it's safe to do so again," he said. "Those things are a hazard."

"My scarecrows aren't hazards!" Odessa rushed into the room, Storm hot on her heels.

I stared at them. "Did you also sneak in through the grate?"

Odessa glanced at me. "Of course. I sent Raphael in first to make sure it was safe to do so." Her gaze shot around the room and she frowned. "Oh! What did you do to Raphael?"

"Your scarecrow tried to kill Olympus," I said. "Monty saved him by... um, well, you can see what he did."

The huge leopard stood and shook out his fur, then trotted over to Odessa and Storm. "I'm at your service. Do either of you give good belly rubs?"

Olympus groaned. "Leave them alone."

Monty ignored him and wagged his tail.

Odessa grabbed a piece of pumpkin off the floor, a scowl on her face. "Is this really all that's left of Raphael? He was such a great scarecrow. You could have told him off rather than ripping him apart."

"He wasn't playing nice," I said. "It was either Olympus or Raphael."

"I know who I'd have picked," Storm muttered. "Why were you stopping us from getting inside?"

"Because you're not welcome here," Olympus said. "I've repeatedly told you everything I know, but you keep coming back and demanding different answers. It's getting you nowhere, other than closer to being arrested for public nuisance and harassment. And I should add sending in an attack scarecrow to kill me to the list."

"No, no! I told Raphael this was a reconnaissance mission only. Although maybe that was too big a word to use. My scarecrows are simple creatures. I didn't instruct him to hurt you, but he must have seen something he didn't like."

"I know exactly what he saw." Storm glowered at Olympus. "What's going on in here? What are you hiding?"

Olympus glanced at me. "If you have a problem with the way I'm doing things, file a formal complaint with the Magic Council."

Storm's top lip curled. "And I'm sure as head of said Magic Council, that complaint will be fairly looked at."

"Of course it will."

"He's not in charge of all of it," I said swiftly. "Just some of it. Um... although I'm not actually sure what Olympus does. What do you do for the Magic Council? I know you're in charge of bits of it, but which bits?"

"You're not helping." He fixed his steely glare on Storm and Odessa. "If this is about Indigo—"

"It is. There's a problem. We've got an emergency on our hands, and we need her back immediately. She'll know what to do."

"What's the emergency," I said. "Have you located Luna?"

"You know Luna?" Odessa said.

"Um..." I looked at Olympus.

He simply shook his head and wiped pumpkin off his shirt.

Storm strode over and grabbed me by the collar. "What do you know about our missing friend? Did you have something to do with her disappearance? It's weird how you appeared out of nowhere and have been so quick to poke around in everyone's business."

"It's not weird. I was hired to do a job. Why shouldn't I be here?"

"I've been asking around about you. No one knows anything about you."

I struggled in her grip, but Storm wouldn't let go. "That's because I'm new to the village. What's your point?"

"I don't trust you. There's something off about you. And you're hiding something, just like he is." Storm jerked her head at Olympus. "If you had anything to do with what happened to Luna, you'll be sorry you ever stepped foot in Witch Haven."

My friends were too on the ball to not notice something was odd about this set up.

Olympus sighed. "I give up. I don't know why I bothered to try to keep you alive and out of jail. Whatever I do, you'll find a way to mess it up."

Ouch! That stung more than it should. "Olympus, maybe we should tell them what's going on."

"Tell us what?" Odessa hurried over and stood beside Storm. "Are you involved with what happened to Luna? You'd better tell us the truth. I have plenty more scarecrows who'd be happy to rough you up."

"No! I didn't take Luna. But I am here to help you find her."

"Why would you do that? What's in it for you?" Storm said.

"Olympus, I'm going to tell them," I said.

He raised his hands in a signal of defeat. "Do what you like."

I pried Storm's fingers from my collar. "It's me. Indigo. I'm in disguise."

Odessa's eyes widened, and she stared at me. "How do we know it's really you? This could be a dark magic trick to distract us from finding Luna."

"When you were eight years old, you ate three pumpkin cream pies all to yourself. You barfed bright orange goo all over Magda's yard."

Odessa gasped. "I did do that!"

"I was there, trying to clear up the mess before anyone found out." I looked at Storm. "And you used to sneak into Pippin Jaggers yard, steal her stone gargoyles, and rearrange them around the village. It used to send her crazy trying to figure out why they kept moving."

Storm's eyes narrowed. "You could have overheard that from anyone."

"No, I couldn't. Only the three of us and Luna knew about that. You swore us to secrecy with our secret handshake."

"Show me the handshake," Storm said.

I held out my hand. After a second of hesitation, she took it. I did two normal handshakes, a finger tap in the middle of her palm, and then tapped the tips of our fingers together.

"It is you!" Odessa threw herself at me and squeezed me tight. "What are you doing? Why do you look like that? Where have you been?"

I looked at Olympus, but he was having no part of this. His back was turned to me and his shoulders hunched.

"After Olympus arrested me, rather than taking me to the Magic Council, he brought me here. He came up with the plan to disguise me. This way, I can keep looking for Luna and figure out what the dark magic wants with this village."

"Oh! That's a genius plan," Odessa said. "We should have thought of that. Although I wouldn't have turned you into an angry goth. Those leather pants..."

"It's not that clever. We were close to figuring it out. I knew something was off about you." Storm gave me a fist bump. "You've been way too nosy and interested in our business to be anyone other than Indigo."

Olympus loudly cleared his throat.

I ignored him. "I tried to keep away, but when I saw you getting in trouble with the Magic Council, I had to help. I didn't want you getting arrested because of me."

Odessa hugged me again. "I'm so glad you're here. But can I still be angry with Olympus for taking you?"

I repressed a grin. "Go right ahead." I looked at my familiars, who'd been silently watching the exchange. "Hey, everyone. Am I forgiven?"

Nugget swished his tail, Hilda tapped her legs on the floor, and Russell fluttered out his wings.

I walked over to them and knelt. "I was doing this for the right reasons. If I walk around looking like myself, I'll be arrested or attacked by the villagers. This way, I can keep doing good work."

"You should have told us," Nugget said. "We're your familiars. We would have helped."

"I... yes, I should have done. I'm sorry."

"You can blame that on me," Olympus said. "I told Indigo to keep quiet about her transformation. The more people who know, the more likely it is that the secret will get out. I shouldn't have wasted my breath. Indigo does whatever she likes." He still sounded annoyed with me.

Hilda climbed onto my shoulder. "We're not angry with you, but we are disappointed you didn't trust us enough to tell us what was happening."

I felt like a total heel. She was right. I should trust them with everything, but I was still new to having familiars, and was feeling my way through this situation. So far, I'd done a lousy job.

"I shouldn't have left any of you out. I regret that. And I've really missed not having you around."

"We missed you, too," Hilda said. "But from now on, don't exclude us. How can we perform our roles as your familiars if you hide things from us?"

I hung my head. "You can't. I won't mess up again."

"I'm a hundred percent sure you will," Nugget said. "But at least we're here to steer you back to the right path when you make a mess of things again."

I held out my arm for Russell to perch on. He took flight and landed on it before sidestepping up to my shoulder. He gave me a sharp tap on the top of my head with his beak.

"I know, I'm an idiot."

"Wait a minute. This story isn't over. That hideous leopard invaded our home!" Nugget's narrow-eyed gaze was fixed on Monty.

Oh, great. That was another thing I needed to confess to. "About that. I needed to get access to Magda's journals. Monty was my distraction while I grabbed them."

"I told you someone had been in the house," Hilda said to Russell and Nugget. "After we'd chased away that oversized kitty, I could smell something was different."

"Sorry again. That was me. I couldn't risk any of you seeing me. I wasn't sure I'd be able to keep quiet about my disguise, or that you wouldn't see through it."

"We really need to work on our familiar witch bond," Hilda said, a disapproving note in her voice. "This isn't how it's supposed to work."

"I will. I'll be an excellent witch to you from now on."

"But that leopard's not sticking around," Nugget said. "There are no vacancies for the role of familiar."

Monty bounded over and licked the top of Nugget's head. "We can be friends. I love other cats, even though you're tiny. And I promise, I won't eat you."

Nugget reared back and hissed. "Get your stinky head away from me. I don't need friends like you."

"Nugget! That's not nice," I said. "Monty's a sweet familiar. And he's already bonded to Olympus, so he's not looking for a new home."

Monty looked up at me and wagged his tail. "I'm the sweetest familiar ever made. Maybe you could share custody of me with Olympus. You give better belly rubs than him."

"Belly rubs!" Nugget growled and stalked away.

I shook my head and laughed. He'd get over it once I'd stocked up on his favorite breakfast treats. I looked around the group. "So, what's the emergency? You came here because you said there was a problem. Is it corpse related?" I gestured at the three skeletons who were sitting watching the show.

"We know nothing about the walking dead." Storm walked over and prodded one of the corpses.

"It is about Luna," Odessa said. "And we've had terrible news."

I swallowed, my throat tightening. "She's not... dead?"

"No! At least we don't think so." Odessa grabbed my hand. "Albert is planning Luna's burial. He wants to hold a ceremony to strip her of her magic so he can claim it as his own."

My mouth dropped open. "He can't do that."

"Technically, it's within his rights," Olympus said. "Another magic user can absorb a dead witch's ability if permission has been granted."

"Luna's not dead," I said. "If her magic is ripped away using this ceremony, it'll destroy her. This has to be the darkness messing with Albert and forcing him to do this."

"Which is why we have to stop him," Odessa said. "We were thinking we could kidnap him."

"Or kill him," Storm said.

"Killing's a little extreme," Odessa said.

"We could always drug him, like he did to us," I said.

"Ooohh! Drugging's an option. We didn't think about that." Odessa nudged Storm. "I told you we needed Indigo's input with this."

"How did you find out what he's planning to do?" I said.

"I went to the bakery first thing to grab a pink sprinkled muffin."

"I told her not to, given the last time Albert saw us he tried to have us burned at the stake," Storm said.

"My sweet fix wouldn't wait. And I know he's just employed a new assistant, so I hoped she would serve me. Anyway, it was so weird. Albert has no memory of attacking us. In fact, he was his usual delightful self. That's when I learned of his plans for Luna's burial."

"He was the same with me when I went to the bakery," I said. "Of course, I was in disguise, but I asked a few questions about the darkness in the village, and he acted like nothing was going on. Although he got a bit threatening at one point. I could see the darkness peeking through."

Storm's mouth twisted to the side. "I still think a blunt force approach is the best option. Take out Albert and the problem is solved."

"No! We can't do that. Where will I get my sweet treats from if we kill Albert?" Odessa shook her head. "There has to be another way."

I chewed on my bottom lip as the others debated how to tackle Albert. Was I ready to face this darkness so soon? My magic still felt like it was evolving. If I messed this up, Luna really could die and the darkness would win.

I glanced at Olympus. He was having nothing to do with this conversation and looked downtrodden and exhausted.

Sympathy fluttered through me. His missing daughter must be on his mind. Of course, he'd always be thinking about her, and I had promised I'd help get him justice. Maybe he thought I'd already forgotten about her.

"You two figure out a plan. Although just to be clear, I'm on Odessa's side. Albert doesn't need to die," I said. "Give me a minute. I just need to speak to Olympus about something."

They both nodded, and continued discussing kidnap and murder options, while I headed over to Olympus. "Hey! I didn't mean to mess up our plans by telling them who I am. And I'm keeping the disguise for now."

"Maybe you won't get to keep it. I should remove the magic. You'll do something to reveal to everyone who you are soon enough, and there's nothing I can do to stop you."

"These are my closest friends. They won't make problems for us. And this is a good thing. Now, we've got extra support."

"You've got support. I've just had my life made more complicated."

"Olympus, don't be like that. I haven't forgotten my promise to you. I will help you figure out what happened to Bloom."

He turned to me, and the sadness in his eyes made my stomach tighten. "Of course. But she's my concern, not yours. You have other priorities. It was selfish of me to expect you to halt the search for Luna because of that."

"You're wrong. It is my concern, too. Whatever happened to her, we'll find out and make them pay."

He nodded, not looking convinced by my words.

"Have you had any more messages sent through about her?"

Olympus sighed, then shook his head. "Nothing new, other than that last note. I keep expecting to find out what my orders will be. What will I have to do to get my daughter back?"

My gut clenched. "I imagine you'd do anything."

"Most likely. Which is why I need you around to make sure I don't do anything I'll regret."

I squeezed his arm. "I'm not going anywhere. And don't give up on me. I will help you." I looked at the corpses. "I just have a few things to sort out first."

"Don't worry about the corpses. I'll deal with them," Olympus said.

"Thanks. And I'll figure out what's going on with the dead in Witch Haven. But... Luna. She's at risk of losing everything. If Albert carries out his plan, there'll be no way to get her back. It'll be like she's been turned into a shadow. She'll have no power."

"Of course." His expression softened. "Get out of here. Go save your friend. And maybe while you're doing that, this whole village."

Chapter 6

After more discussion with Storm and Odessa as to what to do about Albert, and making sure the corpses remained under guard by Monty, we headed to Magda's house. Olympus remained behind, claiming work duties, but I got the impression he didn't want to be around me.

I couldn't dwell on that. I'd made him a promise and I wouldn't break it. But we had to prepare for battle and make sure Albert failed in his attempt to take Luna's power.

"Do you know when Albert's planning this magic transfer ceremony?" I said to Storm and Odessa as we hurried along the quiet streets.

"He's doing it tonight," Odessa said.

"Tonight! That gives us barely any time." Panic welled up in my throat. I had to be focused, and couldn't let my magic go wrong.

"It's taking place in the cemetery," Storm said. "He's even had a plot arranged, and plans to bury some of her favorite things in place of her body."

I shuddered. Luna's wellbeing was hanging in the balance. I couldn't mess up, but my powers were still so new that I didn't entirely trust them. Did I dare test my unstable ability on my best friend?

Odessa gripped my elbow. "We'll do it. We'll stop Albert. We won't let him take Luna from us."

I nodded, her confident tone easing my worries. "I actually feel sorry for Albert. He's being messed up by dark magic."

"And it would break his heart if he truly realized what was about to happen to Luna," Odessa said.

"That's the problem. Albert doesn't see anything wrong with what he's about to do. This darkness has been creeping in so slowly, that people haven't noticed the changes. They've gotten used to the weird vibe, the freaky magic, the disappearances, and the strange behavior going on all around them. And no one blinked an eye when Eden vanished. It was just like another day in weirdsville. Who cares about a young witch going missing?" Storm gasped in a breath and glanced at me.

Odessa hummed a note of sympathy under her breath. "It was a horrible time."

"I heard what happened to Eden," I said to Storm. "I'm really sorry. But I'm sure everyone cared when she went missing."

Storm huffed out her anger. "A few did, but their interest soon faded. Now, it's like she never existed."

"I've always been around to help," Odessa said. "I'll never give up on you."

Storm gave her a tight smile. "Yeah, no matter what I do, I can't shake you loose."

Odessa wrapped an arm around Storm's shoulders. "I'm stuck to you like someone rolled me in superglue and threw me at you. I'm never letting go. They can try to tear us apart, but they'll fail. We're glued together for life."

"You're so weird," Storm muttered, but the smile on her face was wider.

Odessa kissed Storm's cheek. "So are you. We're weirdly compatible. Your weirdness fits my weirdness. We're the weird gang." She grinned at me.

We were a bit weird, but all our odd little pieces fit together just right. "You got no help from the Magic Council to find Eden?"

"I reported it. I demanded they help, and they did the basics, but they weren't that interested. The case is still open, but no one's working on it."

"Have you asked Olympus for help?"

"Hardly! I don't have the luxury of a high up Magic Council member to bend to my will."

"Storm! That's not fair." Odessa thumped her in the arm.

Storm shrugged. "They seemed tight back there. Is there something you want to tell us, Indigo?"

"Um... no. But I am interested in hearing more about Eden."

"Nope. I'm done talking about her." Storm looked away.

Odessa gave me a discreet shake of her head, warning me off of pursuing this topic.

Storm tended to go from calm to nuclear in a few seconds, so I knew when to back off. But this conversation wasn't over.

"Tell us about Olympus," Odessa said.

I glanced at her. "What do you want to know about him?"

"Everything! What's going on with you two? Are you living together? Is it official?"

"Nothing is going on. And no, we're not living together, although I have been hiding out in his office. He let me stay. Olympus is just helping me out."

"Why would he want to do that?" Storm said. "The guy's a massive jerk. And he works for the Magic Council. You hate them."

"Olympus can be a bit of a jerk. And it took me awhile to trust him. And you're right, given where he works, he's basically my enemy."

"So why didn't you blast him with magic and get away after he arrested you?" Storm said.

"Because he gave me breathing space when the Magic Council was debating my fate, he's gotten me out of several scrapes since I've been back, and... he's got his own issues going on. I want to help him with those if I can."

"Do you mean Bloom?" Odessa said.

I nodded. "Olympus hasn't given up hope that Bloom is still out there. And he received a message recently that said someone has her."

"Could that be true?" Odessa said. "It's a long time to kidnap someone and not ask for anything for her safe return. It's been years since she went missing."

"Olympus thinks it's the same witch coven that messed with me and Magda. They're back and causing trouble."

"Or they never left." Storm waved a hand around.

"It makes sense to assume they've been lurking in the background all this time. They started with Magda, and have been waiting for a chance to attempt another takeover," Odessa said. "They've been testing the boundaries over the years to see what they can get away with."

"And hurting villagers while they do that," I said. "The ghosts in Luna's apartment, Albert being weird, the hexed dolls I encountered in Ursa's house."

"Bloom going missing, and Eden," Odessa said. "It could all be a part of the same complex puzzle."

"It's the build up to something big," I said. "The coven is getting ready to take over now everything is so chaotic. People are weak, and won't be ready for any attack."

"Is that why there were corpses in your office?" Odessa said. "Are they part of this dark scheme?"

"Their reanimation could be a side effect of what's going on around here. Silvaria Digby reported the dead have been rising and wandering around the cemetery. And in my disguise as Indy Archer, I was dispatched to see what was happening. Those three corpses followed me home."

"Oh, the walking dead is nothing new. I've had problems with corpses for a while," Odessa said. "They keep chasing my scarecrows."

"Why are they doing that?"

"I have no idea, and I haven't been able to catch one to interrogate. My scarecrows aren't fazed by them, though. They see it as a game and chase the corpses right back." She laughed.

We arrived at the house, and everyone went inside. My familiars settled in their favorite positions, Russell on his perch in the corner of the living room, Hilda by the magic cabinet, and Nugget on his pile of old towels.

I breathed out slowly as I walked through the rooms, a smile on my face. It felt so good to be home.

I stood in front of the magic cabinet and pulled it open. "We need something with power to neutralize what Albert's about to do."

"I'm still in favor of the killing option," Storm said. "Take him out and the job is done. Luna won't be under threat from her evil uncle anymore."

"He's only temporarily evil," Odessa said. "We can all get a bit like that when we're having a bad day."

"Albert doesn't deserve to die," I said. "But if we can't get him to see sense, we need magic to prevent him from completing this ceremony."

"Something to neutralize him without it being terminal." Odessa peered over my shoulder into the magic cabinet. "Look! You've got a jar of fossilized hornets." She took them out of the cabinet. "I wonder how much sting they have in them once they're reanimated."

I eased the jar from her hands. "Let's not find out. Magda collected all kinds of things over the years. This cabinet was her pride and joy. She kept everything she cherished most in here." I brushed my hand across the surface, happy tears in my eyes as I recalled the joyful hours I'd spent in front of this cabinet with my stepmom, learning spells and charms.

Odessa wrapped an arm around my shoulders. "She was amazing. Come on. Let's get hunting for ingredients."

We spent an hour sorting through the magic items in the cabinet and pulling out things that could be useful.

I selected bundles of herbs and other dried ingredients to create a draining spell, a neutralizing spell, and a spell to make a person lose focus.

After everything was assembled, I stepped back and surveyed my collection with Odessa. "What do you think? This should defuse the magic and weaken the strength of the spell Albert plans to cast."

"I vote we shove Albert in the grave he's made for Luna and put an end to this." Storm was lounging in a chair, her feet on the coffee table. "No magic required."

"How about instead of you being so grumpy, you go and make us all some herbal tea?" Odessa said. She looked at me. "She's been a proper grouch since you disappeared."

"I have not," Storm said.

I grinned at her. "Did you miss me?"

"Of course not." Storm climbed to her feet and stomped into the kitchen.

"She absolutely did miss you," Odessa said. "But you know what Storm's like, she hates showing her emotions."

I looked over to the kitchen and smiled. Storm might keep everything buttoned up tight when it came to her feelings, but we were good friends.

Sometimes, these things didn't need saying, you just knew it was true.

"You know, I've been thinking about Limpy," Odessa said.

I slid her a glare. "Are you interested in him? I believe he's single."

She whacked my arm. "No! Not for me, but for you. When you get past the officious Magic Council veneer, he's a good man. He could be good for you."

"I... I'm not so sure. I mean, it's Olympus Duke. He stands for everything I hate."

"You don't hate the Magic Council, you've said that yourself. What they did to you and Magda was wrong, but..."

I nodded. "But they thought they were doing the right thing. And I thought they were for a long time, too. But right now, they're standing in my way, and Olympus is heading up that organization. Well, at least a part of it."

"Don't you think he's even a tiny bit attractive?"

"Sure, he's a good-looking guy."

"There you go. That's a great start."

"A relationship is built on a lot more than looks," I said. "Can I really trust him?"

"Has he ever done anything to deceive you?" Odessa said. "For example, has he ever disguised himself as a different person and hidden from his best friends because of some misguided opinion it was the right thing to do?"

I grimaced. "That's a good point and well made. I really thought I was doing the right thing."

Storm marched back into the room with three mugs of steaming coffee that looked like they were strong enough to stand a spoon up in. "I hate herbal tea." She jabbed a finger at me. "And you do too much thinking. Olympus isn't my type, but I guess he appeals to some. And he's sticking up for you when you need it. Maybe he's not such a jerk."

"Limpy is a decent guy. We all know he's had a few problems in the past. I think you'd be great together," Odessa said.

"How about we focus less on my love life, and more on putting together this magic neutralizing kit and all the spells we need for tonight?" I was eager to stop talking about my never-going-to-happen love life with Olympus.

"I'm just saying, you could do a lot worse." Odessa clapped her hands together. "Right, let's put together some amazing magic to blast Albert off his feet, and make sure Luna keeps her abilities."

I grabbed a mug of coffee and took a sip, grateful the attention had shifted away from Olympus. That was one mystery I wasn't ready to solve.

The rest of the day was spent creating and testing strong magic neutralizing potions, along with draining spells to make sure they were perfect. Nothing could go wrong tonight, not when Luna was counting on us.

I yawned and blinked my eyes. Performing magic was tiring, even when you were just testing out spells.

"We need a recharge before we head out and tackle Albert." Odessa sat on the floor and gestured for us to join us.

"I'm happy on this chair," Storm said. "And I know what you're going to try to make us do."

"You do not!"

"You're going to force us to meditate."

"Oh, perhaps you do. But meditation is perfect. It'll ground us and give us strength. You both take my hands. I'll lead."

I didn't mind a bit of meditation now and again. I settled on the floor and looked at Storm. "Are you joining us?"

"Nope. I'll sleep here. You go right ahead with your chanting and heavy breathing."

"Meditation isn't sleeping. It's about connecting with the energies that keep us powerful. It helps us to be awesome witches," Odessa said.

"I'm awesome enough as it is."

Odessa grabbed a cushion and threw it at Storm. She blasted it apart before it could reach her.

"Hey! Less killing my cushions. Storm, get your behind down here and join in," I said.

"My magic doesn't need a recharge," she muttered.

"It does. You've done just as much magic as we have today. You don't want to fail Luna because you didn't open yourself to a world of inner calm." Odessa leaned over to me. "Storm doesn't like silence because she has to listen to her own thoughts, and they're often dark."

"I heard that."

"So come join us. Prove me wrong, oh dark and mysterious one."

With a dramatic sigh, Storm rolled off the chair and sat with us. She caught my eye and scowled. "This is such a waste of time."

"Be nice. I'll begin," Odessa said. "Using magic comes at a price. If we don't have any down time to soak up the vibes in Witch Haven, ours spells will misfire or we'll be too weak to have any effect on Albert."

"Speak for yourself," Storm muttered.

No one spoke for several minutes as we did the grounding and heavy breathing Storm so despised.

She did have a point. When you were alone with your thoughts, it could get scary, especially with the past I had. But after about ten minutes, I relaxed and let myself feel the magic of the village. I could also sense Storm and Odessa's energies, both shining brightly, although Storm's was an icy blue, whereas Odessa's shone with a pumpkin orange glow.

Something soft and warm slid onto my lap. I opened one eye to find Nugget snuggling down.

"I'm soaking up the vibes, too," he said.

We were soon joined by Hilda and Russell, who took up position on my shoulders.

With my friends and familiars surrounding me, I'd never felt so safe and happy. There really was something to this bonding business.

The sun was just setting as I pulled on my jacket, and we gathered up the supplies we needed for tonight's trip to the cemetery.

Hilda was perched on my shoulder, Russell was already flying around outside, and Nugget waited on the front porch for us to leave.

I didn't feel ready, but there was no time to waste. Luna was in danger, and I'd do whatever I needed to, to make sure she didn't get in even more trouble.

"Come on, gang." Odessa looped her arms through our elbows. "Let's go stop our friend from being ghosted."

Chapter 7

We'd only been in the cemetery a few minutes before an uninvited guest appeared. He was tall, thin, and only recently dead. He wore a smart gray suit that matched the tinge to his skin. The corpse groaned when he saw us and held his arms out.

"There's one of your corpses looking for a hug," Storm said as she set out the magic items she carried.

"They probably only like to come out after dark," Odessa said. "They could be self-conscious about the way they look." She waved at the corpse.

"We could do without these distractions." I shooed the corpse away. "Go back to your grave. We don't need any help."

He simply stared at me.

"And there's another one." Odessa's nose wrinkled. "She looks like she's been in the ground for a while."

A raggedy looking, bony skeleton with the remnants of a black dress covering her bones dragged her way toward us.

"We don't need an audience of corpses watching," Storm said. "They'll give away our location. Albert will know something is wrong the second he arrives if there's a crowd of gaping corpses hanging about."

I looked around to locate my familiars. Nugget was snoozing on the ground, Russell was perched in a tree overhead preening himself, and Hilda was on my shoulder.

"How do you three fancy doing some corpse rustling?" I said.

Nugget snored loudly.

"I know you're awake." I prodded him with a finger.

"I'm not. I'm in a deep sleep. Leave me alone."

"Why don't you show these corpses back to their comfy coffins?"

Nugget rolled over and opened one eye. He stared at the corpses. "They don't smell so good. I'll pass."

"Of course, if you don't want to do it, I could see if Monty is free. He's always obliging, so long as he gets a belly rub."

Nugget jumped up and growled. "Don't let that overgrown kitten in here. He'll mess things up. Come on, we have corpses to deal with." He stalked away.

Hilda tapped me on the cheek. "You shouldn't tease Nugget. He's sensitive about his size, and meeting Monty has given him an inferiority complex."

"Nugget has a big enough ego to make up for his mini size. Would you mind helping him with the corpses?" I said.

"Of course. Can you do the honors? I could do with a size boost to make sure they don't accidentally step on me." Hilda scuttled to the ground.

I pressed a finger on her back, and she transformed into a huge spider with long hairy limbs and impressively terrifying fangs.

I looked up at Russell. "Do you need a magic boost?"

He flew around my head and then shot off toward the corpses.

"I guess not." I sat back on my heels and looked around the cemetery. "Maybe whatever Albert's doing to get access to Luna's magic has troubled the corpses. It's a powerful ceremony. If he's already started his preparations, it could have stirred up trouble."

"Or it's that twisted witch coven thinking it's fun to mess with the dead," Storm said. "That's what I favor."

"Yes, that too. They could be using the corpses to distract us from something else." I shuddered and rubbed my hands up and down my arms. What could be worse than the walking dead? An angry dragon? A gang of goblin berserkers? Maybe an army of furious pixies?

"Someone's just walked through the gate," Odessa whispered. "It's Albert."

"And he's not alone," Storm said. "He's brought friends to watch him destroy his niece."

Albert led a procession of six magic users along the path. I recognized a few, but not all of them. They wore long red robes, and each carried something in their hands, although I couldn't make out what it was.

We'd set up close to the graves, concealed by a neatly trimmed evergreen bush, so we just needed to wait for Albert and his buddies to get closer, before we began our interference magic.

Albert stopped at the head of an open grave. He watched his small group assemble around him, before raising his arms. "Thank you for joining me this evening. I'd like to welcome you to the burial of my niece. Luna has been lost to me for some time, so I've decided to offer her a place of rest and make sure her energy can continue through me."

There was a murmur of agreement from the group.

Storm hissed softly under her breath. "This guy is out of his mind."

I had to agree, but I didn't think it was his fault.

Albert continued. "I've given each of you something of Luna's to place in the ground. These items will identify this spot as hers and help me channel her magic. Everyone, please take a moment to secure your item in the grave, and then we'll begin the evoking spell to draw her energy close."

"I'd like to shove him in that hole and make sure he never gets out," Storm muttered. "Look at him, he's smiling."

"Just remember, Albert's not himself. We all know how much he dotes on Luna."

"It still doesn't seem right to me," Storm grumbled.

Each member of Albert's entourage took it in turns to place an item of Luna's in the grave. I couldn't see them all, but I spotted her favorite pink sweater, a purse she loved to carry around in the shape of a chocolate cupcake, and a book.

Once they'd all placed the items in the grave, they returned to their positions around the edge and looked at Albert.

"We need to time this just right," I whispered. "Let's wait until he starts casting his magic, so we only blunt that. We don't want anything else getting in our way."

"Like the magic animating these corpses," Odessa said. "Have you noticed, their numbers have grown since Albert arrived?"

I'd barely registered how many corpses were lurking around, but she was right. There were a dozen shambling about the cemetery.

"Albert's not paying them any attention," I said.

"Is that because he knows why they're here, or he doesn't care?" Storm said. "Maybe he's only interested in getting his hands on Luna's abilities."

"They've linked hands," Odessa said. "They're about to begin."

And so were we. We were using a combination of spells to neutralize Albert's attempt to take Luna's essence. We had a neutralizing spell to blunt the power of any magic he cast, a draining spell to weaken him, and a confusion spell so he'd have trouble focusing.

"You go first, Odessa," I whispered. "Let's make it hard for this group to concentrate."

She gave me a thumbs up. "I'll add some of my powdered pumpkin to the mix. That'll make things even more intense."

"We shouldn't mess with the magic at this late stage," I said. But I was too late. She'd already pulled a small bottle of powder from her pocket and sprinkled it into the spell mix. She poured the spell into her palm and blew on it, sending the magic straight toward Albert and his group.

I could just see the faint outline of the spell as it swirled around, covering each of them in turn.

Several of the group stepped back and dropped their hold on the others hands.

Albert also looked around. He blinked and swiped his hand down his face.

"It's working," Odessa said. "I knew my powdered pumpkin would give it the right boost."

One of the corpses nearby groaned and lurched at Storm.

She shoved him away. "Keep your hands to yourself. Indigo, where are your familiars? They need to deal with this lot."

I looked around and spotted them herding a large group of corpses on the other side of the cemetery. "They already have their paws and claws full."

"I don't like the look in these corpses' eyes," Storm muttered. "They don't seem so friendly anymore."

I glanced at the corpses again. They didn't look happy, but then they were decaying bone bodies who'd been forced out of the ground. They didn't have much to be happy about.

"Albert's group is still going," Odessa said. "It's time for spell number two."

Storm was in charge of this spell. After a glare at the corpse wobbling its way toward her, she uncorked a bottle full of neutralizing magic and tossed it in the air, before evoking a gust of wind and sending it straight at Albert's group.

Just like the first spell, it coated them, and they sagged under the weight of the magic.

"Something's wrong," Albert said, his gaze darting around. "I'm still not sensing Luna. She should be approaching us by now."

"That could be my fault," one of his group said. "I don't know what's wrong with me tonight, but I'm struggling to remember the words of the spell."

"Me, too," another member of the group said. "Perhaps you should try a simpler spell. One we can all manage. Why not just try talking to Luna?"

"No! That won't work. I need her energy. If we use a different spell, Luna won't return. It has to be this one. Let's keep going, everyone. And concentrate. If you keep getting distracted, this won't work."

"They're a determined bunch," Storm said. "Any time you want me to throw a lightning bolt at Albert, just say. He's the ringleader. If I take him out, the others won't carry on."

"We've still got one more spell up our sleeves," I said. "It's time to drain this group and stop any magic they cast from working."

I'd just uncorked the vial of magic and was about to cast my spell, when Odessa gasped and grabbed my arm.

"I've just seen Luna! She's appeared behind Albert."

Storm was already moving. "Come on! We need to get her before they do." She went to dodge around two corpses standing in her way. They growled and grabbed her.

"Hey! Get off her." I raced to Storm's aid, but before I could reach her, I was seized from behind. I dropped the spell bottle as rotten breath blew across my cheek, and the corpse who'd captured me sucked on the side of my face.

Odessa yelped as she was headed off by three feisty female corpses.

I struggled in the corpse's tight grip. "Eurgh! Stop sucking on me! And don't you dare bite me." I wiggled out of the painful grip and turned to face my attacker, quickly seeing this moldy guy wasn't on his own. There were five more corpses heading straight for me, and they looked mad, just like the scary zombie creatures your mom always told you to run away from.

Odessa squeaked, and a blast of her magic shot past my head.

I turned to see her pinned to the ground as a corpse snapped what was left of his teeth in her face.

What had gotten into these things? Thirty seconds ago, they'd been happy to amble about and watch what we were doing. Now, they were looking at us like we were their new favorite chew toys.

"We have to get Luna," Storm yelled. "Albert's seen her and he's moving in." She blasted a corpse away with her magic and tossed another one over her shoulder.

"You go. I'll hold off the corpses," I said.

Storm only made it a few feet, before a corpse shot out of the darkness and barreled into her, sending her flying into a huge stone crypt.

Odessa was back on her feet and charging toward Storm, blasting bright orange magic at the corpse.

I looked at Albert and his group, and my heart stopped. They'd finished the spell, and although a couple of them were looking uncertain as to what to do next, the rest were focused on Luna's wispy essence. They were about to get her. If Albert made contact with Luna's energy, he'd claim it as his.

I needed the draining spell, but I'd dropped it when I'd been grabbed by the corpse. I looked around and groaned when I saw it spilled over the dirt. It was contaminated, and no use now.

I'd have to tackle Albert and his group with my own magic. I conjured a fireball and held it over my head. "Albert Black! You need to stop."

His head jerked in my direction. "Why? This isn't your business."

"What you're doing is wrong. Luna is still alive. You can't take her magic." I advanced on the group, making sure to keep them all in my sight line.

"What's it got to do with you?" His attention returned to Luna's essence, and he reached out to her.

"A lot of things. I can't let you hurt Luna. If you do this, she'll never come back to Witch Haven."

"You're talking nonsense. She's here right now. And I intend to take her magic." Albert lunged at Luna's energy. He'd almost reached her when a corpse appeared and tried to bite him.

Albert yelped and backed away, blasting out a shower of sparking magic that flickered for a few seconds and then died.

I tilted my head. If the corpses were attacking him, maybe he wasn't involved in making them rise.

"Get to Luna!" Storm yelled from under a pile of corpses.

I reached the group, keeping the fireball alight as a warning to anyone thinking of making a move to grab her.

"Stop the ghost hunter," Albert yelled. "This has nothing to do with her."

A couple of the group moved forward, but the rest stood back, their eyes wide as they watched the chaos grow.

I hurdled a gravestone, taking the quickest route to Luna. I hoped the inhabitant beneath my feet wouldn't be offended, but this was a life or death matter.

I was almost within touching distance of her, when a mass of crimson mist shot out of the darkness. It enveloped Luna's spirit, and they vanished.

The scent of rot filled my nose and a cascade of dark feathers fluttered around me and settled on the dirt. A shimmering wave of red shot across the cemetery as the scent drifted away.

I stood there, my breath heaving out of me as I stared at where Luna had been. What just happened? There was something about that mist, something that tugged at the back of my mind to remember.

"What did you do to my niece?" Albert had escaped the corpse and grabbed my shoulders. "You have no right to interfere."

"I had every right. She's my—" I stopped from revealing who I really was. "You don't know for certain Luna's dead. If you take her energy while she's alive, the damage will be impossible to reverse."

He growled in my face. "You know nothing about my business. Keep your ghost hunting nose out of it. This is a family affair, and we don't want outsiders interfering." After giving me a shake, Albert shoved me away and hurried back to the group.

They stood around talking for a few minutes before walking away. I watched them leave the cemetery, before jumping into the grave and collecting Luna's things. I wasn't leaving them here, in case Albert came back and tried again.

After a quick check to make sure Odessa and Storm were handling the corpses, I pulled myself out of the grave and stared into the darkness.

Something had grabbed Luna. It was as if it had been waiting for the moment she materialized. But what was it? And why was it so interested in preventing Luna from getting back to us?

I knelt and picked up a couple of the black feathers and tucked them inside my jacket. Maybe they'd help me figure out what had Luna in its clutches.

"Indigo! We need help over here," Storm yelled. "We've got more corpses incoming."

I raced over, but then slowed as something growled in the darkness.

A huge hulk of a corpse appeared from behind a crypt. Its bony hands were clenched into fists and its teeth were bared as it lumbered toward me.

I backed away. "Nice corpse. You be on your way. I want no trouble from you."

The corpse kept approaching, and it kept on snarling.

"Back off, unless you want to be a bone pile on the ground." I sparked warning magic on my fingers, but it didn't deter it.

"Don't say I didn't give you a chance." I dropped Luna's things and blasted magic at it.

Although the corpse stumbled back, it kept on coming. Jeez! It was strong, like a skeletal cage fighter.

I grimaced as a hollow ache filled my stomach. I'd already used most of my magic fighting off corpses and Albert, and could feel myself drained. Even my amethyst necklace wasn't glowing and warm.

I kept backing away. "I'm sure you've got a nice, cozy coffin waiting for you. And you deserve a rest. I'm just going to collect my friends and we'll be on our way." I lost my balance as I hit a headstone, and the next thing I knew, I was falling.

The corpse attacked, swinging its huge arms at me.

I rolled out of its way as it fell toward me and whacked my head on another gravestone. I was scrambling away on my hands and knees, my head throbbing and my heart pounding, when there was a thud, and bones crunched together.

That sounded like someone just got squished. I rolled over to see Olympus tackling the corpse. He had it in a headlock and they were rolling around on the ground.

I pulled myself to my feet and staggered toward them. "What are you doing here?"

Olympus held down the corpse and blasted it with a spell that shattered its bones. He stood and brushed down his clothes. "I'm watching your back so you don't get yourself killed."

"I hadn't planned on getting killed, but thanks for the save. I don't know what's gotten into these corpses. All of a sudden they—" I yelped and staggered back as a huge black blur slammed into Olympus and took him off his feet.

My eyes re-focused, and I stared in disbelief as a huge, drooling black dog pinned Olympus to the ground, its teeth clamped around his neck.

Olympus caught my gaze, and panic flared in his eyes.

"Fire Fang! Get off him." Storm raced over and attached a sturdy leash to the dog's collar. "You were supposed to stay home."

"Does that dog belong to you?" I said.

Storm glanced at me. "No. Well, only temporarily."

"I didn't know you had a dog." Fire Fang still had its teeth firmly around Olympus' neck.

"It's a long story. And he's not a dog, he's a hellhound."

"Will you get this thing off me?" Olympus grunted out.

After a brief tussle, Fire Fang let go of Olympus and let Storm drag him away. He was an enormous beast, and must weigh over seventy pounds of pure hellhound muscle.

Olympus gripped his neck and staggered to his feet.

I hurried over to give him a helping hand, but he brushed me away.

"I hope you have a licence for that thing," he muttered to Storm.

"This *thing* isn't mine. And he's not supposed to be out. I left him at home. He must have followed me."

Fire Fang's eyes glowed red, and he growled at Olympus.

"How's Odessa doing?" I said.

"Not so great. One of the corpses knocked her out," Storm said. "She'll be okay."

I looked around. The corpses were moving away. Although they were still grumbling and angry, they were no longer looking for a fight.

I heaved out a sigh. Albert and his posse had fled, Olympus had been bitten by a hellhound, Odessa was unconscious, and Luna had been spirited away by some unwelcome intruder.

This evening had been full of chaos and failure. And it wasn't over yet.

Chapter 8

"We need to regroup," I said. "Figure out this mess and see what our next move should be."

Fire Fang lunged at Olympus again.

"I'll have that creature taken to the pound and destroyed if you can't keep him under control." Olympus eyed the hellhound warily.

"He's fine. He just gets high-spirited when he meets new people. Or people he doesn't like, or people who breathe. Basically anyone," Storm said. "Don't make eye contact and he probably won't bite you."

"He almost chewed through my throat," Olympus said.

Storm shrugged. "It's his way of saying hello. And he only broke the skin. You got lucky. He was reacting to you being so close to Indigo. He knows when someone is trouble."

Olympus sucked in a breath.

I held up a hand. "Let's gather everyone up and go back to Olympus' office. It's the closest place to here. We need to sort through what just happened. And I don't want to hang around in the cemetery any longer than needed, in case the corpses are just taking a rest and regrouping."

Storm and Olympus nodded, although they still glared at each other.

I dodged past a few corpses, who seemed content to amble around the cemetery again and not launch any unprovoked attacks on us. But something had stirred them up. Could that something have been Albert and his gang? And Albert was often around when trouble happened. I needed to look into that when I had a moment to think straight.

I hurried over to Odessa. She was face down in the dirt, her hair splayed out around her. A corpse was sitting on her back.

"You need to find somewhere else to rest that bony behind." I helped the corpse up, and deposited it a good distance away from us, before returning to Odessa. I rolled her carefully onto her back and brushed dirt off her face. She had a huge red mark on the side of her forehead.

"Hey, how are you doing? Ready to wake up?"

Odessa groaned, and her eyes flickered open. "I always say that being too thin is bad for you. The corpse who got me was clearly starving. He took a bite out of my arm." She held up her wounded arm.

"Let me deal with that." Although I was exhausted from pumping out so much magic, I wasn't leaving Odessa in pain. I placed my hands either side of the bite and evoked a healing spell.

"Did we get Luna?"

"Nope. We were close, but something took her." I gave Odessa a rundown of the chaos. "And just after Luna was taken, this awful smell appeared."

"You mean from all the dead bodies racing around?"

"No. This was something else. Apart from the corpses, did you smell anything funky before you passed out?"

Odessa shifted up onto one elbow. "Was it like something dead had been warmed in the sun?"

"Yes! Just like that."

"I got a whiff of something gross when that corpse was chewing on me. I thought it was him, but it hit me like a wave and then vanished. What was it?"

"If the smell was anything to go by, nothing good." I looked around. "Maybe it was a side effect of the magic Albert was doing, but it blasted out just after Luna was grabbed. I thought it might have been from the red mist."

Odessa lifted her nose and took a big sniff. "It's definitely gone now."

"Let's hope it doesn't come back."

It took a good ten minutes for my healing spell to work, but the wound was knitting together, and soon, only a red mark would be left.

I sank back on the ground, my head pounding. I needed a break from doing any more magic or I'd also pass out.

Olympus, Storm, and Fire Fang had joined us, and so had my familiars.

Russell held a bone between his beak and kept squawking and making it whistle.

I eased it gently from his beak and used what little magic I had left to return Hilda to normal size. "Great job, everyone. Those corpses really had it in for us."

"They're not the only one." Olympus glared at the hellhound.

"Who's this?" Nugget said, walking over and sniffing Fire Fang.

"Be careful," I said. "He's not friendly."

Nugget jumped on Fire Fang's back. "He doesn't seem unfriendly to me."

Fire Fang looked uncertain as he glanced over his shoulder at Nugget, but he didn't bite him, so I took that as a good sign.

I helped Odessa to her feet and wrapped an arm around her waist. "Let's get out of here, before the corpses take another shot at us."

My mud-smeared, bloodied group stumbled out of the cemetery and over to Olympus' office.

"So what's with Fire Fang?" I said to Storm. "You've never been into having pets."

"He's not a pet," Storm said.

"He is. And he's a wonderful pet," Odessa said.

"Where did you get him?"

"Oh! Let me tell the story," Odessa said.

Storm gestured at her. "Go ahead. It's not exactly exciting."

"Do you remember, Storm got a job to find a missing hellhound? His owner thought he'd been kidnapped because his puppies fetched a lot of money."

"I remember," I said. "Is this the hellhound?"

Storm shook her head. "No, I got him back to his owner."

Odessa swatted her arm. "I'm telling the story."

Storm held up a hand and smirked at me.

"There were more dogs that had been stolen," Odessa said. "I've got several at my farm, but we found owners for the rest. Apart from Fire Fang."

"He was a stray?" I said.

"I guess so," Storm said. "And he's a mixed breed. He's part hellhound and part I'm not sure. He sometimes does weird things like levitate."

"We couldn't abandon him," Odessa said. "And if we'd given him to the supernatural pound, they'd have put him to sleep." She glared at Olympus.

He nodded. "It's what happens to all dangerous animals. And the ones without owners go first. The place is overrun at the moment."

"Exactly. The poor little guy wouldn't have stood a chance if we'd handed him over. So Storm adopted him."

"No. He's not adopted. He's on a very short term foster with me until I figure out a permanent solution for him."

Fire Fang looked up at Storm and licked her hand.

I smiled. "He looks pretty settled to me. You should rethink not keeping him. You've never settled on a familiar. Maybe Fire Fang could fill that gap. And the company would do you good."

"I like my own company well enough. And I've got no room in my life for a slobbering great hellhound who floats and steals from my cookie stash."

"I like him. Especially since he doesn't mind me riding on his back," Nugget said.

"Then you adopt him," Storm said.

Nugget looked up at me, a hopeful glint in his eyes.

I shook my head. "You don't want me to share custody of Monty, which means we don't have room for Fire Fang."

"Monty is different," Nugget grumbled. "He's so full of himself with all that glossy fur and big fangs. He's such a show off."

"Just like his owner," Storm said.

The comment earned her another glare from Olympus, but he didn't say anything.

We arrived at Olympus' office, and he let us in. Everyone collapsed on the chairs or lounged against the desk, all too exhausted to move or speak.

I dragged myself into the back room, switched on the kettle, and hunted around for food. I needed feeding up and rest after that magical battle.

Olympus joined me, silently putting out mugs for everyone.

"Are you sure that hellhound bite is okay?" I said.

"I'll live. I'm not sure that thing should though."

"It was an accident. Maybe Fire Fang just needs better training. And he's the perfect attack hellhound. Give him the right guidance, and he'd be unstoppable."

"That's my concern."

I made strong coffee for everyone, despite the late hour. We all needed a jolt of energy. "Have you got any cookies?"

Olympus hunted around, and found a couple of packs of cookies, and we headed back to join the others.

Monty and Fire Fang were eyeing each other with great interest. Nugget was still perched on Fire Fang's back with a smug look on his fuzzy face.

"If he gives you trouble, you have my permission to bite him," Nugget said to Fire Fang.

"No one is biting anyone," Olympus said.

Monty wagged his tail. "I love having all these new friends here. Even the spider doesn't seem so scary now we've been properly introduced." He licked Hilda.

She tumbled over and rolled away, leaving a trail of leopard spit behind her.

I scooped her up, dried her on my jacket, and settled her on my shoulder. Monty could be clumsy, and I didn't want Hilda getting stepped on.

No one spoke for several minutes as we gorged on cookies and drank coffee.

"We got one thing right tonight," Odessa said. "Albert failed. He didn't get Luna's magic."

"But something took Luna's energy. I'd almost reached her when she was whisked away," I said.

"Tell me what you saw," Olympus said.

"It was a red mist. And it's not the first time I've seen that mist in Witch Haven. When we were attacked and put on the pyre, the mist was floating through the crowd. It felt stronger tonight, and it was aimed straight at Luna. The mist enveloped her, and then they vanished, leaving behind a load of feathers and a foul smell." I reached into my jacket and pulled out the feathers I'd picked up.

Russell squawked. He flew at the feathers and yanked them from my fingers.

"What's wrong with you?" I said.

Russell dropped the feathers, then blasted magic at them. They exploded in front of us.

Hilda tapped my cheek. "He thinks there was something bad about them."

Russell continued to caw and flap around.

"He said they're not safe to be around. They were full of darkness," Hilda said.

"I guess that's no surprise, given where they came from," I said. "They're not connected to Albert. Although... has anyone else noticed he's always around or involved when bad things happen?"

Odessa chuckled. "You can't think sweet Albert Black is at the heart of this village's problems? He's a cuddly, harmless old baker."

"Is he? Could that be a disguise? Albert was the first to discover Luna gone from the hospital. He drugged us and almost got us burned, and now he's trying to get his hands on Luna's power."

Storm shook her head. "I'm with Odessa. Albert is being used. He's not masterminding these troubles. He's not smart enough, or powerful enough. His power lies in creating the perfect cream puff, not apocalypse zombies and rancid mist."

I didn't disagree. Albert was so... ordinary. "What if he tries to take Luna's power again?"

"Maybe the chaos in the cemetery has put him off," Odessa said. "With the weird magic whizzing around, the corpses running about, and then you attacking him, he won't be keen to go back there again."

"You attacked Albert?" Olympus glared at me.

"I know. I should have kept hidden," I said. "I almost blew my cover."

Olympus gave me a pointed look, but didn't say anything.

"I still can't figure out why the corpses turned evil?" Odessa said. "One minute, they were happy to do a bit of moaning and groaning, and then it's as if someone flicked a switch. They started grabbing us." She rubbed the spot on her arm where she'd been bitten.

"Something triggered them," I said. "Again, I'm going to come back to Albert. Did he set them off?"

"It's not Albert. Maybe they activated when a certain spell went off nearby," Storm said.

"Or they felt threatened by something," Olympus said.

Everyone was quiet as we mulled over the corpse problem.

"Did you get close enough to Luna to speak to her?" Odessa said.

"I didn't, but she looked confused to me. That's no surprise, given what Albert was doing."

"So we're back to square one," Storm said.

"Not quite. Albert didn't get what he wanted," Odessa said. "And no one died. I call that a bonus."

If it was a bonus we survived the night, then we were all in trouble.

I looked at my familiars. Fire Fang and Monty were snuggled up together. Nugget was lounging on Fire Fang's back, and even Russell was getting involved, and snuggling down on top of the furry heap.

I yawned and rubbed my eyes. I needed rest, too.

Olympus nudged me. "How about we call it a night? No one's in any shape to do much more tonight."

I wanted to figure out our next move when it came to Luna, but my head was aching and my eyes were blurry. "How about we meet here tomorrow morning? We could all do with a recharge. We get sleep and then figure out this mess."

"That sounds good to me," Storm said. "I'll walk you back to the farm, Odessa."

"No, you're good. I'll summon my boys. They can escort me home." She leaned out the door and let out a piercing wolf whistle.

Storm extracted Fire Fang from the pile of slumbering familiars, and we said our goodbyes before they headed out.

I turned to Olympus. "Since the cat is pretty much out of the bag about who I really am, I may as well go back to Magda's house. There's no reason for me to stay here."

His forehead wrinkled, then he nodded. "Of course. If you don't want to stay."

"No, it's not that. I just don't want to get in your way. This is a small place, and I've already overstayed my welcome."

"Here they are," Odessa said brightly. "My handsome escorts to take me safely home. I think I'll get them to carry me. My legs won't hold out for much longer, I'm so shattered."

Two large scarecrows loomed into view and shoved their way into the office.

"Are you sure you'll be okay on your own?" I said to Odessa. "I could always come back with you."

Her eyes widened, and she shook her head, before shooting a meaningful glance at Olympus. "I'll be just perfect. You two have fun." She waved goodbye, hopped into one of her scarecrow's arms, and they all headed out.

I looked at the door, and then at Olympus. "I should get going, too."

"You've still got some things here. If you don't want to walk home, I don't mind if you stay another night. It's no bother. And, just so you know, you're never in my way."

It was tempting to take Olympus up on his offer. And weirdly enough, I felt odd leaving him. I'd gotten used to having him around, making sure I was eating, teasing me, and checking up on me. It had been a long time since anyone had done that.

I shook my head. "Thanks, but I've been missing my old bed, and I really need a good night of sleep. Plus, if I don't go back with my familiars, they'll think I've abandoned them again."

"Of course. I'll see you back here tomorrow." He reached for my hand and gave it a gentle squeeze.

"You can count on it. Tomorrow everything will look better. We'll figure out what happened at the cemetery, make a new plan, and finally get Luna back. Then we can tackle everything else."

He walked me to the door, and we said our goodbyes. I headed out with my familiars, stumbling with tiredness as we walked back to Magda's house.

No one said anything, and as we got inside, we all went straight to our beds.

The second my head touched the pillow, I sank into a deep and much-needed sleep.

Chapter 9

It's amazing what a good night of rest can do. I'd gotten a solid ten hours of uninterrupted sleep and was recharged and ready for action.

I looked out my bedroom window at the bright morning, happy to be back in my old house. Maybe I'd missed Olympus a tiny bit, but it was so good to have my favorite pillow and my warm snuggly blankets tucked around me.

I had a quick shower and got dressed, then headed down the stairs. I was surprised I hadn't been disturbed by any of my familiars in the night, but they must have been tuckered out by all the excitement in the cemetery.

I headed into the living room. Russell had his head tucked under his wing and was still fast asleep. Hilda was nowhere to be seen, and Nugget was snoozing on his pile of towels in one corner.

I snuck past to the kitchen, not wanting to wake them. They looked so cute when they were asleep.

After a quick check through the cupboards, I frowned. I needed to get some food in. I was still surviving on the tinned goods Magda had left behind, and they were ancient. Apart from the occasional food gift from friends, I was running out of options.

I grabbed a tin of peaches and got stuck in while I waited for the coffee to brew.

Nugget mooched into the kitchen, yawning to himself.

"Hey, sleepyhead. Last night was something else, wasn't it?" I said.

He glanced at me. "What did you get up to?"

"Very funny. I thought those corpses would get the better of us. They just kept on coming."

He walked to his empty food bowl and gave it a pointed look.

I lifted a hand. "I get it. No talking until you've been fed." I was much the same until I'd been caffeinated. I pulled out a tin of tuna flavored cat food and served it up alongside a fresh bowl of water.

Nugget got stuck in without another word.

I made my coffee and leaned against the kitchen cabinet. "I've been thinking about what happened in the cemetery. I reckon whatever was in that red mist was waiting for Luna to appear. Maybe she managed to get free from whatever took her from the hospital, but Albert's magic exposed her, and the darkness took its opportunity to get her back."

Nugget made noncommittal noises as he continued to eat.

Russell appeared, soaring through the open doorway. He settled on the countertop and jabbed his beak at the open tin of peaches.

I pulled out a slice and gave it to him. "Good morning to you, too."

He bobbed his head and then got to work on his breakfast.

"We'll finish this, then head over to see Olympus. We need to figure out our next move. And I also need to make it look like I'm actually working for the Magic Council, otherwise this disguise will be rumbled."

Nugget gave me the side eye. He clearly wasn't in a good mood this morning, despite all the sleep he'd had.

Hilda scuttled into the kitchen. She clambered up my leg and onto my shoulder.

"I hope you're in a better mood than these two. They're barely paying me any attention," I said.

"I'm always in a good mood," she said.

"Did you have any bad dreams after our encounter with all those corpses?"

Hilda tapped her legs a few times. "Corpses?"

I smiled at her. "Yes. Sadly, it wasn't a nightmare. And you all did amazing jobs in keeping those shambling troublemakers away from us while we tackled Albert."

Hilda bobbed around on my shoulder for a few seconds. "What are you talking about?"

I laughed. "Good one. I wish it was that easy to forget, but I don't think we've seen the last of that cemetery, or our overly ripe shambling neighbors."

"She's losing her mind," Nugget said. "I knew something like this would happen."

"Hey! That's mean. My mind is just perfect."

"Nugget, that wasn't nice," Hilda said. "Indigo's entitled to have bad dreams, just like the rest of us."

A shiver of unease ran through me. "Bad dreams?"

"It sounds like you had quite a nightmare," Hilda said. "Were the zombies chasing you?"

"In a manner of speaking, but it wasn't a nightmare. We were all in the cemetery last night. We went to stop Albert from taking Luna's magic. When we were there, the undead got feisty. You must remember that."

They were all silent as they stared at me.

I lowered my coffee mug and placed it down carefully. Maybe I was still asleep. I pinched myself, and the pain showed me I was wide awake. "You're all winding me up, aren't you?"

"Are you feeling unwell?" Hilda said. "You could be coming down with something and it's giving you delusions. A fever does that. Do you feel hot?"

"Hilda, tell me you remember last night. What did we do?"

"We stayed here," she said. "We didn't do anything exciting."

I narrowed my eyes. "Do any of you remember going to the cemetery?"

They all shook their heads.

"Have you got more food?" Nugget said.

Russell tapped his beak on the empty tin of peaches.

Something seriously weird was going on here. How could they not remember?

"We should go out and play if our owner won't give us more to eat," Nugget said.

"Owner! You always complain if I say I own you. And we don't have time to play. We have a million and one things to do. Finding Luna being on the top of that list."

"Nugget's right. We should go outside. I can find myself a tasty fresh breakfast out there," Hilda said.

I hurried to the door to block them from getting out. "Everyone hold on. What did you do when we came back here after being at the cemetery? Did you go out? Did you get in trouble? Something must have happened to make you forget what we did."

"Hilda's already said, we didn't do anything. You're the one being weird, talking about corpses and spells, and Albert being strange," Nugget said. "You need to move, unless you want me doing my business on the rug."

I hurriedly stepped away. They genuinely didn't seem to remember. I opened the door and stood aside to let them go out.

They bundled through the door, more interested in playing in the early morning light than dealing with the darkness in the village.

Maybe it was delayed shock. Last night had been full on, and even I was feeling a little tender.

I pulled on my boots and jacket, and walked outside. "I'm heading over to see Olympus. Are you coming?"

"No, we're staying here to play," Nugget said. "Russell's about to start hide and go seek. You can join in if you like."

Nugget never played games. That showed me something was wrong. "I'm good. I'll catch up with you later." I raced away from the house. Could there behavior be a side effect of all the magic that was blasted around the cemetery last night? Although if it was, I wasn't having the same memory lapse.

I dashed to Olympus' office, but slowed as I reached the door and read the note pinned on it. *Gone on vacation. Be back soon.*

My mouth dropped open. Vacation! Olympus wouldn't disappear in the middle of this mess. He wouldn't just abandon me, would he?

I took a step back and tugged on my bottom lip. Had I put too much trust in Olympus, and he'd walked away because things were getting difficult?

I peered through the windows of the office, wondering if this was another joke, but there was no sign of anyone inside.

I raced to Odessa's farm. I was wheezing by the time I got there and leaned on the farm gate to catch my breath.

"Indigo! What are you doing here so early?" Odessa appeared on the top step of her porch, dressed in a fluffy purple dressing gown.

I jogged over to her. "I'm so glad you're here. I was beginning to think I'd entered a parallel universe."

She glanced around. "Everything looks the same to me, but you never know. Have you had any coffee? That always helps me make sense of the world."

"I have, but it didn't do me any good."

"Then you need more. Come inside. I've just taken some cinnamon pumpkin spiced muffins out of the oven. Give them a few minutes, and they'll be cool enough to eat."

I walked up the steps and entered her house. It was an old wooden building, full of the delicious smells of sweet baking, with a faint underlying whiff of pumpkin and hay.

Odessa led me through to the kitchen, and I sat at a small table by the window and accepted a mug of coffee from her.

"What have I done to deserve this visit?" She settled at the table opposite me and sipped on her own coffee.

"I think my familiars' memories have been wiped."

Her eyes widened. "That's terrible. Who'd do such a thing?"

"I have no idea. But I think it has something to do with last night."

Odessa lifted a finger as she jumped from her seat. "Hold that thought. I'll go grab the muffins." She returned a moment later and handed me a huge, bright orange muffin covered in glitter.

"Thanks. I tried to talk to them about what happened, but they don't remember anything. All they were interested in was breakfast and then going out to play."

Odessa tilted her head. "Isn't that normal? I mean, I don't have familiars as such, my scarecrows fulfill that role, but animal familiars are usually food obsessed and playful."

"Sure, but this felt different. They weren't acting like themselves. And it's like the last twelve hours have been wiped from their memories."

Odessa peered out the window. "Oh, look! There's Shamrock. I must introduce you to him again. He thinks you're adorable."

"Ummm... Odessa, I'm not in the market to date a scarecrow."

"You've said that before, but you don't know Shamrock. He's a charmer. And probably my most handsome scarecrow to date. I'm proud of my work on him." She jumped up and whistled out the window. "Hey, Shamrock, get over here. Indigo's arrived." She looked back at me. "Oh, he won't recognize you in your dominatrix disguise."

"Fortunately not. Especially since I'm not in the mood for you to match-make me with an amorous scarecrow."

Shamrock appeared by the window and peered inside. He nodded at me, but focused on Odessa, as if awaiting orders.

She chewed on her bottom lip. "Maybe now's not a good time. But Shamrock likes you. I mean, the real you, not the in disguise you."

I gestured her to quieten down. "Remember, the fewer people who know about this the better."

"Oh, Shamrock won't say anything, mainly because he can't speak. Off you go, Shamrock. I'll come find you later." Odessa gestured the scarecrow away from the window.

He turned and studied me, then raised his pumpkin head and sniffed.

"What's he doing?" I whispered.

"I'm not sure. Shamrock, is something wrong?"

He leaned closer to me and sniffed again.

"You don't think he can smell it's me, do you?" I leaned away.

"Oh! No, I shouldn't think so. Off you go. It's rude to sniff the guests."

Shamrock sniffed again, then loped away from the window.

I took a bite of the muffin and chewed slowly. "There must be a way to figure out what's wrong with my familiars."

"You know, it could be as simple as them getting their days muddled," Odessa said. "It happens to me all the time. Sometimes, I think it's a Monday when really it's a Tuesday."

"They wouldn't have muddled up last night with any other night. It was unforgettable. Albert's twisted magic, Luna appearing, the red mist, and the attacking corpses."

Odessa jerked her head back and blinked rapidly. "What are you talking about?"

I lowered my muffin, and my chest tightened. "You too? You don't remember?"

"What do you mean? Do you want a top up of coffee?"

"No, I don't want anything. Odessa, you were with me last night. We went to the cemetery together. We were with Storm and we planned to stop Albert from stealing Luna's magic."

"Oh! Very funny. This is a joke." She swatted the back of my hand. "Don't tease me when I haven't had enough caffeine. I almost took you seriously for a second."

"Look at my face. I'm not joking around."

Her forehead wrinkled. "You do look serious. But maybe you're the one getting your days muddled. I didn't see you last night. I was here. We hadn't made any plans to see each other."

"We did. And aren't you even curious about Luna? I just told you she showed up in the cemetery."

"No, you told me that you thought she showed up. There's a difference." Odessa's eyes glazed over, and she turned her head. "Are you sure I can't set you up with Shamrock? Once you get past the slightly freaky head and murderous desires, he really is lovely."

"I've got to go." I pushed away from the table and hurried out of the kitchen.

"Wait! You've only been here a short while. Stay for the day, and we can have some fun. I'm carving pumpkins later."

"Another time. I need to see Storm." After a hasty goodbye, I raced away from the farm.

Storm had to remember what happened. I couldn't be the only one with memories of fighting corpses and stopping Albert. I needed someone to confirm that it had actually happened, because I was beginning to doubt myself.

Storm lived in a small apartment in the center of the village, so it didn't take me long to get there, and I was soon hammering on her door.

"Storm, it's Indigo. Are you home?" I kept knocking and then pressed my ear against the door to see if I could hear her inside.

The apartment door next to hers creaked open, and an older woman looked out. "If you're looking for Storm, she's already left."

"Oh, is she working on a case?" I said.

"I don't know. She had a bag with her. It looked like she was going on vacation."

"She wouldn't go away at a time like this," I said.

"A time like what?" The woman's gaze ran over me, suspicion on her face.

"Oh, it's nothing. Sorry to bother you." I hurried away from the apartment block and stood on the street corner. What should I do next?

I glanced at the bakery. I didn't dare risk going in to see Albert, not after I'd confronted him in the cemetery. Although if his memory had also disappeared, he wouldn't remember that. But it felt like too much of a risk.

It also felt like someone or something was taking away my support network, and I couldn't let that happen. No one messed with my familiars and friends and got away with it. Not for long, anyway.

I turned and marched toward the cemetery. That's where I needed to be. That was where it had all gone wrong.

Maybe I'd find answers lurking among the graves.

Chapter 10

Every step I took closer to the cemetery, I became less sure of what I should do. I'd gotten used to having friends and familiars in my life, but now they were being yanked away. With their memories gone, they couldn't help me.

Was this the darkness messing with us, sensing we were close to a breakthrough, so it needed to make sure we failed?

Worry gnawed at my gut like a hungry hamster. I'd sensed a familiarity in that red mist just before it had taken Luna. Did I know the magic users causing these problems?

I shook my head. I couldn't know them. I'd been a teenager when everything had gone wrong. A seventeen-year-old novice witch with my head in the clouds and no clue what to do with my life. This couldn't be a contact I'd made back then.

But I couldn't stop thinking that I knew them. Or maybe they knew me. Had this darkness been following me around my whole life? And I was so used to having it trail behind me, that I felt like we were connected.

My necklace flared to life and warmed my skin. I took it as a comforting sign that I needed to trust myself more. It was better to have people around to help during troubles like this, but I had to figure out what had messed with Odessa and my familiars memories on my own.

I walked through the open wooden cemetery gates and stopped. I took a minute to look around and get a feel of the space, to see if my magic could sense any troubling energies that may have caused the memory loss.

Everything was quiet, as it should be in a graveyard. The wind gently stirred the leaves on the trees, and a few birds twittered around, but other than that, it was peaceful.

I walked over to the grave where Albert and his group had summoned Luna.

There were still a few feathers on the ground as I pressed my hand into the dirt. I got a faint flicker of the stripping magic Albert had attempted to use, but not much else.

I walked around the grave, picking up faint hints of magic. Albert had meant business last night. He'd desired Luna's magic. If that red mist hadn't grabbed her and taken her away, there'd be nothing left of her.

I paused by a crumbling headstone. Was I looking at this the wrong way around? I'd always assumed the mist was making trouble for the village, but what if it saw Luna was in danger and had rescued her?

I shook my head, not convinced by that. Whenever there was trouble, that red mist showed up and stirred it up even more. Maybe it got jealous because it thought it was about to lose something it wanted. It took Luna so no one else could have her.

I closed my eyes and took myself back to the previous evening. It had been chaotic, and I could easily have missed something. The corpses had been jumping at anyone who got in their way, Albert and his group had been using difficult magic that could easily have gone wrong. Then Storm's hellhound showed up and attacked Olympus. It had been one mess after another. And after the mist took Luna, there'd been that weird pulse that had shot across the cemetery. It must have hit everyone. Could that be the cause of the memory loss?

I opened my eyes and let out a yelp, leaping back and hitting a headstone. A short, thin woman with narrowed eyes that glowed purple stood right in front of me.

I crashed to the ground and lay there gasping. "Holy broomsticks! Where did you come from?"

She walked over to me, leaning heavily on a pointed stick. When I looked at it closely, I realized it was a long bone from some kind of animal that had been sharpened at the end. At least, I hoped it was from an animal and not some unfortunate cemetery resident.

"What are you doing in my cemetery?" Her voice was low and gravelly.

"Your cemetery? Are you Silvaria Digby?" I struggled to my feet.

"I might be. What's it to you?"

"I'm Indigo, I mean, I'm Indy Archer. I was hired by the Magic Council to investigate the corpses coming to life. Well, not coming to life, but you know what I mean. The corpses walking around. The undead rising." I waved my arms in the air, doing a passable impression of a zombie.

"You were here last night," she said.

"That's right. Do you remember seeing me?" I was relieved someone else had witnessed what happened. I was beginning to doubt myself.

"Of course I did. You caused a mess. What were you playing at?"

"We weren't playing at anything, Silvaria."

"Miss Digby. You were all throwing magic around like it was cheap candy on Halloween. It'll take me days to set this place right."

"Sorry about that. I was here with my friends—"

"Storm and Odessa?" she said. "They're friends of yours?"

"Yes. And you definitely saw them here with me?"

She scowled. "I have eyes in my head. You were watching Albert and his friends do that ceremony around the grave. He paid me double to make sure it was ready in time. I don't know what the hurry was, it's not as if Luna is even around to go in that hole. But he demanded the grave was dug so he could perform his ritual."

"Did you know what he had planned?"

"It's not my business to question customers. He wanted a hole dug, he paid me for the job, so I did it."

"Albert wanted to take away Luna's magic."

Miss Digby shrugged. "So what? The dead can't do much with magic."

"What if Luna's not dead?"

She glared at me for a second. "It's still none of my business. And I don't want you poking around here anymore."

"You don't want your corpse problem solved?"

"No! I made a mistake filing a report with the Magic Council. I'm better off dealing with this on my own."

"But I'd like to help," I said.

Miss Digby sniffed and adjusted her grip on the bone stick. "Why? What's in it for you?"

"Well, it's my job. And I like this village. I don't want to see it overrun with shambling corpses. And last night, those corpses weren't friendly. One of them bit Odessa."

"That was her fault. She shouldn't have been messing around in here."

I resisted the urge to argue with her. It looked like Silvaria Digby was a glass half empty person.

"Since you saw what was going on last night, did you also see a mist appear? It happened when Albert summoned Luna. It pulsed out across the whole cemetery."

"I didn't watch the whole time. I've got better things to do than waste my time staring at idiots making fools of themselves."

I pressed my lips together. "So you didn't see a red mist?"

"I can't say I did. Now, you should leave. I've got work to do. I need to clear up the mess Albert left behind. And I suppose I should fill in the empty grave, or someone will fall in it and injure themselves. I don't want to have to deal with a claim for compensation because some half-brain stumbled into it."

"No! Don't do that. There could still be useful information here."

She crossed her arms over her chest. "Useful information? What exactly are you investigating? You said you were interested in the corpse problem, but we've been talking about Albert, Luna, and some odd mist you claim to have seen."

"Can't I be interested in both?"

Her top lip curled. "You're the same as everyone else. You say one thing, but you mean another. You're only here because you want to get something."

Silvaria Digby was as spiky as the stick she held. "I really do want to help with your wandering corpses. Why don't you tell me more about them?"

"If you can read, everything I know is in the report I filed with the Magic Council." She shook her head. "I wish I'd never bothered. Waste of time. If you want something done, you do it yourself."

I needed to handle Miss Digby carefully if I was going to get anything useful out of her. "What if you walk me around the place? You can show me where the first corpse emerged. Maybe that's the root of the problem."

"You can walk around on your own if you must, but there's nothing I can show you that'll help." She waved a hand at me. "You get out of my way. I've had enough misused magic in this place to last a lifetime. Go on, get."

"I'll just take a quick look around before I leave. But if you change your mind, I'm happy to investigate the problem. Maybe someone's cursed the place, or is trying to use the corpses to do their bidding. Or maybe—"

"There are a lot of maybes in that sentence and nothing definite. Once you have proof of what's going on, maybe we'll talk. Otherwise, I'm not interested." Miss Digby turned and hobbled away.

"I'll be here if you change your mind. Or you can find me at Olympus Duke's office. Or ask for me at the Magic Council."

Miss Digby glanced at me over her shoulder. "I'll be glad when this whole place is gone, then I'll have nothing to worry about but myself. I may finally get some peace."

I watched as she headed across the cemetery, grumbling under her breath. There was a woman who needed a break from the dead.

My mouth twisted to the side. I hated to admit this, but she sort of reminded me of myself not so long ago. I always refused help, thought the world was out to get me, and just wanted a quiet life where I wouldn't be disturbed. But that way of doing things had gotten me a one-way ticket to lonely town.

Despite Miss Digby's insistence that I leave, I had no plans to go anywhere just yet.

I walked to the spot we'd hidden in as Albert cast his spells and hunted around, but there was nothing useful there. I headed back to the empty grave and walked around it twice. I picked up a couple of the feathers and put them inside my jacket. Russell had been less than pleased when I'd revealed those feathers last night, which suggested there was something bad attached to them. Maybe if I did a reveal spell, it would show me something useful.

I did a slow circuit of the whole cemetery, keeping half an eye out for any corpses that might pop up to say hello, and poking around to find anything to give me a lead as to why people's memories had disappeared.

I stood on something that crunched under my boot. I lifted my foot and looked at what I'd stepped on. It was a piece of broken pottery. I knelt and picked it up, turning it over in my hands as I brushed off the mud.

I sucked in a breath. It was a piece of the ghost jar that had been stolen from my house. I'd recognize the marbled coloring anywhere.

Why would someone bring this into the cemetery? I stared at the piece of ghost jar, then hunted around to see if I could find more fragments. I discovered several large pieces, which suggested someone had either dropped it or it was smashed onto the ground. And once it had been broken, the ghost inside would have been freed.

I looked around, worried I might not be alone. Why would anyone want to set that ghostly monster free? There wasn't an ounce of goodness in either of the ghosts I'd tackled in Luna's apartment.

After I was convinced no malevolent ghost was watching me and waiting to strike, I gathered up as much of the ghost jar as I could find and slipped it into my pocket.

I hurried back to the gates and took one last look at the cemetery. Something dodgy had gone on here, and I wasn't sure I had all the pieces I needed to figure out what that was.

Chapter 11

"It's unnatural for a cat to play fetch with a ball." I scooped up the small ball Nugget kept bringing me to throw for him.

He hopped up and down on his paws. "Play ball, play ball."

I tossed the ball, and he raced off after it.

I shook my head and frowned. Even though watching him chase a ball was adorable, my mood was glum. I'd spent the whole day trying to figure out what had happened at the cemetery and kept drawing blanks.

I'd tried half a dozen spells to get any magic to reveal itself from the feathers and the ghost jar, and I'd gotten zero results. If there'd been any power in these objects, it was gone. These clues had led me straight to a dead end.

My bad mood was also not helped by the fact my familiars were becoming useless. Well, not useless in the sense that they were still adorable animals, but they were behaving like normal pets. Nugget was only saying one or two words, and spent the rest of his time either wanting to play, sleep, ask for head strokes, or demand food. Hilda had spent all afternoon designing an enormous web in one corner of the room and hadn't come over to me for hours. And Russell had spent all day sitting on the roof and didn't seem to want to be in the house anymore.

As well as being frustrated by their change in behavior, I was also worried. These were my familiars. I drew my strength from them, and they helped me when I was in trouble. I wouldn't toss them out if they regressed into being normal, everyday pets, but what was happening to their magic? It felt unnatural.

It must have something to do with the spells cast last night, but I couldn't figure out what that was, or how to reverse it.

On my way back from the cemetery earlier in the day, I'd gone to Olympus' office to see if he'd come back. There'd been no sign of him or Monty, so I'd collected my things and Magda's journals.

Olympus hadn't even locked the door before going off on his supposed vacation. Anyone could have walked in and taken what they liked, but it seemed he didn't care there were confidential files on a desk and his few belongings were still in the back room. Olympus had simply upped and left.

I'd even done a quick check through his things to help me figure out where he'd gone, but everything was untouched. It was like he woke up in the morning, walked straight out the door, and didn't look back.

That was far from normal behavior, given the crisis we faced. Or rather, I faced, since no one else could remember what was going on.

I needed a break from casting magic on the useless clues I'd collected, so I picked up one of Magda's journals and flicked through it, hoping for inspiration and guidance.

Magda had been full of wise words when I'd been growing up. She was never the kind of parent who'd tell me to accept something because she told me it was that way. She always took the time to sit me down and talk things through. When I messed up, which I did a lot, Magda never let me get away with it. But she didn't simply give me a clout and tell me I was an idiot, she'd explain why my behavior wasn't acceptable and that I was letting myself down. Magda used to say that nobody wanted to be remembered for being a giant jerk and a selfish idiot.

I definitely didn't. Although we'd had a few sessions where I'd dug my heels in and refused to see sense, but Magda never gave up on me. She always wanted me to find the right path.

I'd gotten off that path for a long time, but I was back on it now. Although at the moment, it felt like someone had given me a mighty shove in the wrong direction by taking my friends and familiars memories.

But this was a short-term problem, and I would get them back, no matter what it took. I wasn't letting go of everything I'd got. Whatever this dark magic coven threw at me, I'd grab it and sling it right back at them.

There was a sharp tap on the front door. I put down the journal, hurried over, and peered out the window. Odessa stood out there, and she was carrying a large hamper over one arm. She waved when she saw me.

I wasn't in the mood for company, but maybe her memory had returned. I pulled open the door.

"I come bearing gifts." Odessa walked in and headed into the living room.

"Um, thanks. What have I done to deserve gifts?"

"I bet you haven't eaten all day."

"Not true. I ate breakfast."

Odessa arched an eyebrow as she turned to face me and set her free hand on her hip. "We all know what your version of breakfast is. It comes out of a tin and is eaten with your fingers. Anyway, I'm here now, so you don't need to worry about food for the rest of the day."

I sniffed the air and smiled as I inhaled the delicious scents of sugar, spice, and chocolate drifting out of Odessa's hamper. "What did you bring me?"

"All the treats under the sun. And I have so much to tell you."

I settled in a seat and tried hard not to drool as Odessa unpacked pumpkin brownies, orange cookies studded with chocolate chips, and pale yellow blondies with pumpkin frosting.

"Is it about last night? Are you getting your memories back?"

She glanced at me. "You're not still going on about that? It must have been one heck of a dream to make you think it was real."

I let out a soft sigh. "I guess it must have been. The weird thing is, someone else saw us there. So unless I shared the same dream with Miss Digby..." I trailed off my words.

Odessa's eye twitched. "Dream sharing has been recorded for hundreds of years. It's very possible you had a similar dream with someone else. Where are the plates? We can't eat without plates. And we need something to drink. And napkins. You're a terrible host. I haul all these goodies here and you don't even lay out the basics."

I placed my hand over my heart. "I can't have you thinking I'm a terrible host. I might miss my slot in Witch Hostess Monthly." I strolled to the kitchen, grabbed everything she'd ordered, and returned to the living room.

Odessa took the plates from me and inspected them. "That's better. You can't eat perfection if you don't have anything to eat it off."

"I could have eaten it off my hand."

She put a blondie on a plate and handed it to me. "So, do you want to hear my news?"

"I do. But maybe you should hear mine first."

"Mine is much more exciting. And it's true."

"And mine isn't?"

Her eye twitched again as she settled in a seat and took a large bite of cookie. She chewed for several seconds before swallowing. "I'm sure you think it's real, but you've been having problems recently. Perhaps you pushed yourself too hard and something got broken."

I stared at her, my mouth open. "You think I had a breakdown?"

"I wouldn't put it in such harsh terms, but you've had a lot going on. You haven't long come back to the village, you've gotten in trouble with residents, and the Magic Council wants you arrested. And you're living in this crumbling old house that's in serious need of updating."

Several of the windows banged open.

"Careful what you say. This house has feelings." I took a bite of my blondie.

"Sorry, house. But you have to admit, you're looking tired around the edges. I blame Indigo. She should spend time and money on you, and make you beautiful again."

"This house has a perfect rustic charm to it," I said. "And I have been busy. Mainly having a breakdown if I believe you."

"Oh! Don't get offended. I'm only trying to help. Forget I said anything. Anyway, you're never going to guess what I heard."

"That the dead are rising?"

Odessa wrinkled her nose. "No, that's just nasty."

"Or that Luna's uncle summoned her to the cemetery last night and tried to take away her magic essence?"

"Now you're being ridiculous. Are you going to listen to me or not?"

"It depends on if you're going to listen to me," I said. "Something weird is going on here, and you're a part of it."

"If you're not going to be nice, I'll leave." Odessa began packing up the goodies she'd brought.

"No, wait! Don't leave. I am starving. And I did forget to eat lunch." I gestured for her to remain in her seat. "Tell me your news. I promise, I won't interrupt."

She glared at me for a second, before letting out a sigh. "Very well. And my news does have to do with the cemetery."

"Something else has happened there?"

Her sunny smile returned, and she nodded. "I heard the news from several people. It's quite incredible."

I couldn't resist. "Does it have to do with a red mist?"

She tilted her head. "It could do. Although no one mentioned a red mist to me. And they'd probably have described it as a gas rather than a mist."

I shook my head. "A gas?"

"There was an explosion! Apparently, there was a natural gas leak in the middle of the cemetery that destroyed graves and tore up the ground."

I didn't even try to hide my cynicism. "Is that the lie being used to cover up what really happened?"

"It's not a lie. I went and took a look myself. You can't get in the cemetery. It's been cordoned off for repair and cleaning, and the cemetery guardian doesn't want anyone in there until it's safe."

"You saw Silvaria Digby? That's what she told you?"

"No, and you don't ever really see Silvaria. She's only interested in you if you have no pulse. And she's so grumpy that no one wants anything to do with her. But everyone's talking about the explosion. Imagine, it could have been terrible if there was someone in there. They'd have been killed."

"There were lots of people in there when this so-called gas explosion happened. The living and the dead."

Odessa scrunched up her face. "I haven't heard of anyone being injured. Are you sure you've got your facts right?"

I looked at her recently bitten arm and the fading mark on her forehead. "Odessa, do you mind if we try something?"

"Sure. What do you want to try?"

I took the empty plate from her and set it on the table, before taking her hands in mine. "I'm working on a spell. You trust me, don't you?"

"Of course. I know you'd never do anything to hurt me."

"That's right. And this won't hurt you. I'm hoping it'll help. Just don't fight my magic. It may feel a bit weird."

She leaned back in her seat. "I don't like the sound of that. Let's have another cake and we can talk about our next ladies get together. I'm thinking maybe a chocolate making day. That could be fun."

"This won't take long. And I'm sure you'll feel much better after it."

Odessa chewed on her bottom lip, her gaze darting around as if she was looking for an escape route. "Is it a restorative spell?"

"Something like that. It should add clarity to your thoughts." It was a risk, using magic to get Odessa to remember, but if a spell had taken away her memories, I should be able to restore them.

I settled in front of her, opened my power, and our magic joined together effortlessly. The familiar sparkles of Odessa's power intertwined with mine and filled the room with the scent of cinnamon, although it smelt less powerful than usual.

I evoked a recall spell under my breath and pulsed it through Odessa.

Her eyes glazed, and she jerked away from me. "What are you doing?"

"Nothing bad. How do you feel?"

Her eye twitched uncontrollably, and she tried to pull her hands away. "I don't like it. Stop that right now."

"Is it hurting you?"

"No, I just don't like it. Get away from me." Odessa succeeded in yanking her hands away and breaking the connection.

I sat back on my heels and looked at her. "Do you feel any different?"

"Yes, I feel grubby. You shouldn't have used that spell on me, whatever it was. I don't feel any clarity, I just feel queasy. And my eyes feel funny."

Whatever magic was influencing Odessa, it was heavy duty, but I needed to find a way around it. I was tempted to try the spell again, but it seemed to have done more harm than good, and Odessa was still twitching in her chair and looking uncomfortable.

"How about we have another cake?" I returned to my seat.

"Yes, I need it after that." She glared at me as she munched on another cookie.

"Sorry. I really thought it would help you."

"Let's forget about it." Her smile returned, although it looked strained. "Maybe later we can go and look at the cemetery and see the after-effects of the explosion. How exciting. So little happens around Witch Haven."

"You're kidding? Don't forget Luna's still missing."

She frowned. "Oh, yes, of course. We must do something about that."

I studied Odessa as worry grew inside me. "We are. And we will get her back. It's what we've been focusing on ever since she vanished. There's no way we're giving up on Luna."

Odessa patted her stomach. "We must not forget our old friend." She glanced at the pile of Magda's journals and picked one up. "What are these?"

"More of my stepmom's life history. I've been looking through them to see if I can find clues about the dark witch coven."

Odessa wrinkled her nose as she flipped through the journal. "There are a lot of curious poems in here."

"Poems? Magda didn't write poetry."

"They look like poems. Although they also look like..." she laughed, "spells."

I walked over to see what she was looking at. Odessa had turned to a page full of scribbled notes on spells and ideas for how to make them more effective. "That's exactly what they are."

She chuckled. "Of course. What fun. Magda had a real imagination."

"She did." The worry that had been building inside me overflowed. "Odessa, what do you think you're looking at?"

"I'm not sure. It all sounds like fun, though. All these tales of witches, magic, and casting spells. If only it was true."

I pressed a hand against Odessa's forehead. "Are you feeling okay? Maybe I shouldn't have done that spell on you."

"I'm fine. Don't I look fine?" She pushed my hand away. "I could do with another cake, though."

"You look like your normal self, but you're talking as if you don't believe in magic."

Odessa blinked several times and her eye did that weird twitching thing again. "I, um... I'm not sure I do. Is there such a thing as magic?"

"Odessa! You make incredible magic filled scarecrows that terrify the villagers. It's what you're known for. You're so proud of your awesome scarecrows."

Her expression blanked. "Scarecrows? You mean my pumpkin farm? I sometimes make scarecrows for the children, but that's just for fun. And they're never scary. I always overstuff them, so they end up looking chubby and comical."

This couldn't be happening. Not only had Odessa lost her memories of last night, but she now didn't believe in magic. Was this my fault? Had my attempts to bring her memories to the surface sped up her transformation into... a normal person? Was Odessa no longer a witch?

I had to know for sure.

I took the journal out of her hand and leaned in close. "Odessa, cast a spell for me."

She laughed brightly. "You're funny. I wish I could. I'd imagine I was twenty pounds lighter. No, three inches taller, because then I'd be the perfect weight for my height. No, I know what I'd do, I'd cast a spell so all the handsome, eligible bachelors in the village fell in love with me. Then I'd have my pick. Maybe I'd create a spell to make a cupcake that had no calories. Wouldn't that be amazing?"

"You can probably do all of those things. Try it. Maybe something simple, like a light ball. That was one of the first spells we were taught how to control."

"A light ball?" She looked around the room. "You do need some lights in here. It's getting gloomy. I think it might rain."

Panic gripped my insides and made me woozy. "Just pretend you're an awesome witch and can cast any spell you can think of. Close your eyes and imagine doing it. Cast a spell out in front of you and see what happens."

"That seems a bit childish," Odessa said. "We're grown women with responsibilities. We don't have time for games. We have businesses to run. Well, I do. Have you had any thoughts about what you'll do for money now you're back? The refuse collectors are hiring."

"Humor me. Please."

She pursed her lips. "Very well. So I just close my eyes and think about a cupcake with no calories?"

"Try the light spell," I said. "That should work. Anyone can do a light spell."

Odessa looked at me as though I'd lost all reason. Then she closed her eyes, thrust out her hands and said, "light spell."

Nothing happened.

"Give it one more try," I said. "Really imagine a ball of light appearing in front of you."

"This is ridiculous." She lowered her hands. "And you're putting me off my cakes. Nothing puts me off dessert, but you're being so strange."

I wasn't the one being strange. Odessa had forgotten she was a witch. It was the strangest thing I'd ever seen happen.

There was another knock at the door, and I turned toward it. "Don't go anywhere. We're not done yet."

"You're so odd," she muttered under her breath as I hurried to the front door.

I opened it to find Olympus outside. "Hey! Nice vacation?"

He stared at me. "Vacation?"

"I came to see you this morning. You'd put a note on your door saying you'd gone on vacation. And you'd left the office unlocked."

"Err... okay. Maybe I did. But I can't think about anything else right now. I must see you." He barged past me and dashed into the living room.

I shut the door and hurried after him. "What's wrong? Have you got news about Bloom?"

Olympus shook his head. "This isn't about her." He glanced at Odessa. "I was hoping to have a private audience."

"Don't mind me," Odessa said. "Indigo will tell me anything you say to her. We have no secrets. Although I should warn you, she's being a little weird today."

"I love her weirdness," Olympus said. "That's why I'm here. I love everything about Indigo."

I stared at him. "You do?"

"Every inch of you is perfect. From your strange colored hair, to your love of that hairy spider. All I can think about is you."

"Awww! How romantic," Odessa said.

"Is it? Or is it creepy and weird? Olympus, where have you been?"

"On an important mission." His eyes gleamed. "It's taken me hours to get this right. At least, I hope I've gotten it right. That's for you to decide."

"Have you been investigating the corpses?" I said. "Did you get a lead on what's making them stir?"

His smile faltered. "The corpses?"

"Please say you remember last night in the cemetery. You came and rescued me from a corpse. Then you got bitten by Storm's hellhound. Check your neck, you've still got the bite marks on your skin."

His hand went to his throat. "I thought they were love bites. Didn't you give these to me?"

I heaved out a sigh. "Hardly. Listen, something odd is happening to you, and I think magic is involved. You've lost your memory. So has Odessa."

Olympus clasped my hand. "If I have, then I'll make plenty more beautiful memories with you. I want to spend the rest of my life with you."

Odessa sighed. "It's like being at the movies watching you two."

"What movie are you thinking of? Dawn of the Dead? Or maybe Coraline? This day does feel like I've stepped into a parallel universe." I tried to pull my hand out of Olympus' grasp, but he held on tight.

"Both of you need to stop being so weird. We've got a serious problem to deal with."

Olympus knelt on one knee. "I have to know if you can love me. Because if you can't, I don't know what I'll do."

Odessa squeaked. "Is he going to..." she waved a hand at me.

"Get up!" I tugged on his elbow.

"Not until I ask. Indigo, will you marry me?"

Odessa clapped her hands together. "Yes! And you must ask me to be bridesmaid."

"Oh, for broomsticks' sake. Get off your knee. You don't want to marry me." My cheeks grew warm, and I felt mortified.

"I absolutely do. Please say yes and make me the happiest man alive." Olympus fumbled in his pocket and produced a small black box. He opened it to reveal a purple diamond. "To go with your hair. Not this hair, your real hair. When you look like you. Will you accept me?"

I pushed the ring away. "No! I don't even know you that well. And if you had any sense in that head of yours, you wouldn't be proposing when we're in the middle of a crisis."

His expression dropped, but he remained kneeling. "Will you at least think about it? I'd be an excellent husband, and I can provide everything you want. You won't have to live here anymore. You can move in with me. Or we can buy a new place in Witch Haven."

I had to try something drastic to shock some sense back into him.

"You want us to start wedded bliss in a village the Magic Council is thinking of destroying because it's so tainted with darkness? A village where you had your heart broken because your daughter went missing? A place where I murdered sixty-six people? This is where you want our forever to be?"

Olympus simply nodded and grinned at me. "I'd live anywhere, so long as it's with you."

"And you must have plenty of spare rooms in your new house, so I can come and stay all the time," Odessa said. "And of course, you'll need space for a nursery for the little ones."

I clapped my hands over my ears. "Will you two stop! No marriage, no ring, no babies, no house."

"I'll convince you to love me," Olympus said, still on his bended knee. "I'm not giving up. Whatever it takes, I'll find a way to your heart."

I finally got my hand free from him and backed away.

Olympus climbed to his feet and moved toward me. He was staring at my mouth. Was he going to attempt a kiss? If he tried, I'd hit him.

A rush of warm, dirt-infused air swirled around me. Silvaria Digby appeared in my living room. She staggered about for a second, before her gaze locked on to me.

"What the heck are you doing? How did you get through my magic wards?" I said.

"There's no time to explain. You're coming with me." She grabbed me, and we vanished.

Chapter 12

I stumbled to the ground as we reappeared somewhere cold and dark. The ground looked like concrete, and a musty smell of old damp cloth hung in the air.

I glared up at Silvaria. "What's going on?"

"That's what I want to know from you. You have some explaining to do." She scowled down at me.

"You first." I climbed to my feet and brushed dirt from my pants. "Where are we?"

She pursed her lips. "Inside a crypt in my cemetery. It belongs to a family of demi-goblins."

"And how did you know I was staying in Magda's old house?"

"I knew something was off when we first met. You claim to be Indy Archer, an employee of the Magic Council, but you know too much about this place for someone who's just arrived. And all of a sudden, you're friends with Storm and Odessa. Explain that!"

"I... I am Indy. And I do work for the Magic Council. And... my friendship with Storm and Odessa is a new thing." There was a muted thud against the side of the crypt, and I jumped. "What was that?"

"My problem, and the reason I've brought you here." Miss Digby crossed her arms over her bony chest. "Don't lie to me. Your arrival coincided with the disappearance of Indigo Ash. Care to comment on that?"

Eek! It looked like I'd been rumbled. "No, not really. Maybe Indigo is renting her house to me while she... has things to deal with."

"Sure she did. Or maybe you're Indigo." Miss Digby pinched my arm. "What's with the disguise? And don't say you're not wearing one. I felt it when I grabbed you."

"Before I answer that question, have you got an issue with Indigo?" It felt weird talking about myself in the third person.

"Why would I have an issue with her?"

"Because of what she did when she was seventeen. Lots of people remember that."

Miss Digby lifted her chin. "I wasn't here when she, or rather you, blasted this place apart with your stepmom. I turned up a couple of years after it happened. Of course, I've heard the gossip, but I've never been much of a one to listen to idle chatter. I make my own mind up about people."

"And have you made your mind up about Indigo?"

"Usually, people are easy to figure out. They all want something, and will do whatever they have to do to get it. They stomp over people to meet their own needs. Maybe that's what you did all those years ago with your stepmom."

I tilted my head. "I'm still not sure if you have a problem with Indigo."

Miss Digby grunted. "I can't say as I do. I'm sure that'll change once I get to know you better."

"You don't want to toss me into a grave, burn me on a witch pyre, or expel me from the village if I let you know who I really am?"

"I'd only want to do those things if you really annoy me," Miss Digby said. "So, what's with the disguise?"

I held up my hands in defeat. "Okay, so I'm Indigo. And the disguise is needed because the villagers hate me and the Magic Council wants to arrest me."

She barked out a laugh. "You sure are unpopular. And I thought everyone around here didn't like me. I'm glad you came back. I'm no longer the most hated person in Witch Haven."

"I definitely beat you on that score. But I still want to know how you broke through my magic and got into the house." There was another thud against the crypt.

Miss Digby glanced at the stone wall and licked her thin lips. "I'm a guardian of barriers. I monitor the barriers between the living and the dead. I've done this job for a long time, and there are always ways to get through wards and barriers when you know what to look for. And this is an emergency. I needed you here."

"What's your problem? I'm guessing it's related to whatever is hitting this crypt?"

"The problem is, everyone is saying you're responsible for my corpses getting up and walking around."

"I thought you didn't listen to gossip?"

She sniffed. "Only when it suits me. And I've heard it from several sources, most of them reliable. Why would you mess with my dead?"

"I haven't been messing with them."

"You were interested in them when you were poking around the cemetery. Did you think you'd left clues behind and was worried someone would realize you're behind this?"

I rubbed my hands up and down my arms. "I wish I could stand here and argue with you, but I've got a lot going on, and your corpses are now at the bottom of my to-do list. My friends are in trouble. I have to—"

"You have to fix my corpse problem. They were fine before you interfered."

"I can't fix them! I don't know why they're on the rise. Although..."

Miss Digby shuffled closer. "What do you know about them?"

"Nothing for certain, but while you were getting your gossip fix about me, was there any talk of people losing their magic? Or forgetting magic even exists?"

She grunted out her surprise. "I suppose that's your doing too?"

"No, but maybe the memory loss and the dead getting up for a wander could be connected. How many corpses are we talking?"

"All of them."

My jaw dropped and a trickle of fear ran down my spine. "Every single dead body is now..." I waved at the door.

"Yep. It happened not long after you'd done your snooping around. Keep talking. Why do you think this is all connected?"

"Maybe the magic from last night triggered something." I looked at the closed crypt door as several sharp bangs echoed through the chilled interior. "The dead have forgotten they're supposed to be dead, just like everyone who helped me stop Albert and his group has forgotten what happened." My gaze ran over Miss Digby. "Everyone apart from you and me."

"I had nothing to do with that. And I didn't stick around to the end, so I missed the finale."

"There was a pulse of foul smelling magic that flowed out across the cemetery. Everyone was hit with it. It could have seeped into the dirt and made the dead think it was time to wake up."

Miss Digby scrubbed at her chin. "It would take someone with power to influence so many corpses. Did you cast that magic?"

"No, but the thing that took Luna did."

"And you think that's the cause of my problems?"

"It must be. Or it's a big part of it. We can't let this take away people's memories of magic and spell casting, or it really will be the end of Witch Haven. Odessa no longer believes she's a witch, and she doesn't even remember her scarecrows. The change happened so quickly. It was scary."

"That's not my problem to worry about."

"It is if this magic is messing with your residents. They've forgotten they're supposed to be dead. You won't get a second of peace while you try to contain them."

She grunted again. "Maybe so. But we need to deal with these corpses before anything else. The Magic Council hired you for this job, so get to work. I don't care who you are, but you must settle my dead."

I looked around the inside of the cold, solid crypt and dread trickled down my spine. "There's a reason we materialized inside here, isn't there?"

Miss Digby nodded. "Everyone is up and about. And, well, let's just say they aren't happy to be here." She pulled up her sleeve to reveal three large bite marks.

I sucked in a breath. "Silvaria, I promise you, I had nothing to do with the dead rising. This magic is hurting the people we care about, and I'd never unleash anything like that on the village."

"You did once. You could be doing it again."

I lifted my chin and stared her down. "No! Not anymore."

"Maybe I believe that, maybe I don't, but I still need your backup. I can't handle them on my own. Not when they're so vicious."

"You're asking for my help?"

She growled at me. "I'm asking you to fix the mess I think you're involved with. Are you able to do that?"

A loud crash on the side of the crypt made me flinch. "We could stay in here. Maybe they'll go back in their coffins once they get bored."

"No, this rising feels different. I've tried every spell I can think of to get them to settle, but the magic only aggravates them. This time, they're not going down without a fight. Are you with me?"

I gulped. Taking on a cemetery full of angry corpses felt beyond me. But Silvaria must be struggling if she asked for help. "What do you need me to do?"

"Get them to calm down. Use whatever means you have to. I've put a barrier around the cemetery so they can't escape into the village and cause havoc, but I can only hold that for so long. We must reduce their numbers and subdue as many as we can."

"When you say reduce their numbers..."

"Slice, dice, and blast the bones apart."

"Uh, right. Got it."

"Let's go take down some corpses. Follow me." Miss Digby shuffled over and pushed open the heavy crypt door.

The second it opened, moans and groans filled the air.

I peeked over her shoulder and instantly backed away. There were dozens of shambling corpses out there.

"Are you ready?" Miss Digby said.

"Not really."

"Good. Let's go. You deal with the group on the left, I'll tackle the right." She charged out, twirling her bone stick and slamming it into anything that got close.

I snuck out on my tiptoes and edged around the crypt. It seemed disrespectful to destroy these bony shamblers, especially if magic was making them misbehave.

Silvaria yelled a battle cry, and I heard bones shatter. She didn't seem to care much about the skeletons she was supposed to protect. I'd probably feel the same if they'd taken a few chunks out of my arm with their rotten teeth.

I blasted a warning flare of magic at three corpses who were paying me too much attention, but they kept on coming.

"This doesn't need to get nasty," I said. "Head on home and shut the lid when you get there."

They moaned and then charged. Jeez! They were fast.

I dodged around the crypt and came face-to-face with two more bony attackers. I slammed a knockback spell into them and leaped over their bones as they hit the ground.

I spotted Miss Digby dashing across the cemetery, a group of corpses chasing her.

Teeth clacked too close to my ear, and I hit the dirt just as a huge corpse dressed in a decaying black suit grabbed me.

"Not today, my friend." I blasted him away and staggered to my feet. If I kept getting involved in fights like this, I'd need to enrol in ninja witch school.

"Indigo! Get over here," Miss Digby yelled.

I dodged through the skeletons in various states of stomach churning decay and ran toward her. My heart raced as I saw her surrounded by the dead.

I knocked a few away as I approached. "Run!"

"I can't. And my magic is fading. I'm exhausted," she gasped out. "I'm using too much energy to keep the barrier in place. My spells are losing focus."

A few corpses got too close, and I shoved one away and blasted the others with a fireball.

"Keep fighting," I yelled. "They have to slow down soon."

Miss Digby slumped down and heaved out a breath. "I give up."

"Don't do that!" I pushed away a corpse. "You can't stop now. Their numbers are thinning, and some are staying away from us. They've seen what will happen if they don't."

"I can't go on." Miss Digby pinched the bridge of her nose. "I never wanted to be a cemetery guardian."

I grabbed a corpse in a headlock as it tried to grab Miss Digby and flung it away. "Get up! Don't give up now. If you do, they'll definitely beat us."

"It was my parents' fault. They were cemetery guardians and insisted I go into the family business." She shook her head. "You know what I wanted to be?"

"How about alive? That's good enough for now." I blasted more magic at the corpses and sent a group of three flying away.

"I wanted to be a dancer. I wanted to travel the world and make people spellbound with my incredible moves. It'll never happen now, not with my dodgy hips."

"You'll have dodgy everythings if these corpses get their hands on you. Silvaria, on your feet. Keep on fighting."

She glanced up at me, and the resignation in her eyes was clear. "Why? If I let the corpses take me, I can finally let go. I don't have to pretend to be something I'm not."

I glanced at her. She sounded a lot like me. I'd once been that cynical until I'd learned that things could change and get better if you opened yourself up to the possibility.

"You could join an amateur dance troupe. You can still dance while doing your duties here." I hit a corpse in the chest with a fireball. It burst into flames and staggered away, slamming into more corpses and sending them tumbling.

"It wouldn't be the same," Silvaria said. "Everyone would laugh at me. The skinny, bony old woman limping around and shaking her bits that have no legal right to be shaken."

"Who cares if they do laugh? Don't let other people's opinions of you stop you from doing what will make you happy." I raced forward and rammed into a corpse, before slamming it to the ground. I rolled around with my moldy, ripe friend for a few seconds, before shattering it apart with a spell.

I kicked a corpse that got too close, then jumped up and raced back to Silvaria. "You can change your life. You can make it better. But you'll only do that if you stand up now and help me."

She struggled to her feet and glanced at me. "It's too late for us. We should let the corpses take us."

My head whipped around. "Take us where?"

"Anywhere is better than here. They can eat us, bury us, or do what they like with us."

"Maybe that works for you, but I've not given up yet." I heaved in a breath and my head spun as I inhaled decay and dirt. I would have to admit defeat soon. I was pulling double duty in my attempt to defeat these corpses, and they just kept on coming. "Silvaria, use your magic!"

She held up a hand and a pale trickle of magic fell to the floor. "I'm done."

I gulped in air. "How many dead are buried in this cemetery?"

"A few hundred, if you don't count the double graves."

"I do. Silvaria, if you don't use your magic to protect yourself, you might as well be dead. I promise, if we get out of this, I'll find you a dance school, and I'll even come to the first lesson with you. We can shake our bits together to the loudest music we can find and not give two flying figs what people think of us."

Her eyes narrowed. "Why do you want to help me fulfill my dreams?"

"I don't exactly want to, but you dragged me into this mess. I'm trying to save our butts and give you something to live for." I blasted out a knockback spell. It took out a few corpses, but some of them weren't affected as the power of my spells weakened.

Silvaria rolled her shoulders and a glint of determination entered her eyes. "Maybe this is the wrong fight."

"It could be, but we need to finish it, before it finishes us," I said. "Are you with me?"

She stepped away, shook her head, and vanished.

"What the..." If Silvaria was leaving, so was I. I cast a transportation spell to get me the heck out of corpseville. Nothing happened.

I wrestled with a corpse for a second, and once I got free, I tried again. My magic was weak, but I should have one last big spell left in me.

I was about to cast again, but hesitated. Silvaria had put a barrier around the cemetery, and she was probably the only one who could get in and out. That sneaky, mean-spirited cemetery guardian. She'd brought me here knowing I wouldn't be able to escape.

Curses flew from my lips as I got whacked on the head by a hard, bony arm.

I was on my own with these skeletons, and I'd have to fight them until my magic wore out and I became corpse food.

I'd just sparked a raggedy looking fireball in my hand, when there was a guttural roar from behind the crowd of corpses pressing in on me. Something huge with an orange head charged through them, shattering bones and flinging them in all directions.

I lowered my fireball. It was Shamrock!

He smashed, thumped, and plowed his way through the corpses, until he reached me.

I stared at him, my mouth open. "That was incredible." I squeaked as he grabbed me and threw me over his shoulder in a fireman's lift.

"Hey! I'm good. I can walk. You don't need to carry me." I squeaked again as Shamrock rocketed away, slammed through several more corpses, and headed to the gates.

Chapter 13

I was bumped and jostled on Shamrock's shoulder as he raced to the wooden gates of the cemetery. He was like a super athlete, dodging and weaving to avoid the corpses. And when he couldn't get out of their way, he slammed through them like a professional linebacker.

I raised my head and saw that the corpses left behind weren't pursuing us. Maybe they'd learned it was better not to tangle with an angry scarecrow on a mission to save the witch he was besotted with.

"You can put me down, Shamrock. We're good. No one is chasing us."

He didn't let go as he barreled toward the gates, and I could do nothing but hold on tight and hope he'd tire.

I yelped as I was abruptly jerked off his shoulder. Shamrock staggered back and lost his hold on me. I hit the ground and rolled over until a headstone stopped me.

My eyes widened as I pulled myself up and tried to figure out what had happened. Shamrock was flat on his back, one arm bent at an unnatural angle, and one side of his wonderful pumpkin head smashed in as if he'd just hit a brick wall. I grimaced. Or rather, an invisible magic barrier no one could see.

I scrambled over to him. The light was still blazing in his eyes and he made a groaning sound.

"Hang in there. I'll get us out." I stood and hurried to the gates, but before I could reach them, my fingers met invisible resistance I couldn't push through. Yep, this was one strong magic barrier making sure we weren't getting anywhere fast.

I hurried back to Shamrock, wincing at how badly he'd been mangled. "We'll get you fixed up once we're out of here. I just have to figure out how to get through this barrier." I did a quick look around to make sure the corpses weren't paying us attention, but it seemed like they'd had enough. There were some still shambling around, but they weren't heading our way.

I went back to the barrier and tested it. The magic was holding fast. Silvaria had meant business when she put this in place. But I'd find a way through. I had an injured scarecrow who needed medical attention. And I had to hope Odessa could repair him. Perhaps this is what she needed, a prompt to remind her what an awesome witch she really was.

I drew in a deep breath, let it out slowly, and centered my magic, focusing on bringing down part of the barrier. The magic sparked and wavered, but I was exhausted and my magical battery was drained. I needed time to recharge, and the energy in the cemetery wasn't the best source to use. After all, almost everything in here was dead.

I returned to Shamrock, sat next to him, and patted his shoulder. "Thanks for saving me from the corpses. But I have to ask, how did you know it was me?"

He beckoned me closer, and as I leaned down, he sniffed me.

I jerked back. "You know what I smell like?"

Shamrock nodded his damaged head. That was kind of creepy, but also interesting that I had a unique smell. Well, unique to this scarecrow.

"Don't go anywhere. I'm going to see if I can find where Silvaria keeps the supplies. She could have something useful we can use to carve a hole through her magic."

Shamrock attempted to crawl after me as I hurried away, but after some encouragement, he flopped back on the ground.

I hunted around the cemetery, looking for anywhere Silvaria might store her magic equipment. Most magic users used items to channel or charge their magic, but all I found were shovels, a well-used pickaxe, and something that looked worryingly like a bone saw. Maybe she used her bone walking stick as her energy channel, or she was using the bones of her residents to draw power. I shuddered. I was definitely not being buried in this place. I didn't want anyone shaping my bones into a handy walking stick.

After a thorough search of the cemetery, I came up empty-handed. I emerged from behind a large tree and yelped as I came face-to-face with four corpses.

They groaned and stumbled toward me. I backed away, not wanting to get into another magic fight. I still had a little power left, but I needed to save it so

I could figure out a way to get out of here and help Shamrock.

"Nice walking dead. There's nothing to see here. You head back to your coffins. I expect you could do with a lie down after all this excitement."

They didn't seem to agree and kept groaning and shuffling toward me.

I dodged to one side as one of them made a grab for me. My heel caught on something and I lost my balance. I flapped my arms to stay upright, but suddenly I was falling. And rather than hitting the dirt, I kept on falling.

I groaned as I landed on my back and something crunched beneath me. I scrambled up and looked around. Holy broomsticks! I'd landed in an open grave. And I wasn't the only occupant.

My body shuddered at the feel of the slimy, itchy energy leeching off the skeleton I'd hit. My teeth chattered and all the warmth left my body.

I staggered to my feet and took a second to get my bearings. The grave I'd landed in had been dug so deep, I couldn't see over the top.

But at least the corpses hadn't followed me in, although I could hear them groaning and shuffling around nearby, but they were staying away from the grave. Maybe they could feel the dark vibes emanating from these bones, just like I could.

I gingerly toed aside a leg bone and found a patch of dirt that had no bones on it. The second I was no longer in contact with the skeleton, I felt better. The ice in my veins thawed and my head cleared.

Were these bones the cause of the problems in the cemetery? They looked old and there was no clothing or hair, suggesting this person had been dead awhile. Could they have been cursed and then placed in this grave? Had someone sneakily dug this hole here and deposited these evil bones to make the dead stir?

I couldn't leave them here, or they'd keep causing problems. But I also didn't want to touch them.

I wrapped the sleeves of my sweater around my hands and grabbed a pile of bones. They vibrated in my fingers, not seeming happy that they were being moved.

It felt disrespectful, but I shuffled the rest of the bones around with my feet. Maybe they needed to be in a particular order for the magic to work.

I threw the bones I'd grabbed out of the grave, but I kept being drawn to the skull. I didn't want to look at it, but it was like I had no choice.

"You're doing this, aren't you," I said to the grinning skull. "What do you want to mess with these nice corpses for? They've done nothing to you."

The skull continued to grin at me.

"Well, since you've got my attention, I'll take you, too. No biting, though." I grabbed the skull and heaved it over the top of the grave. The second I moved it, the energy changed, and the sinister atmosphere faded.

Great. It had to be the skull. The creepy, leering skull that was the problem.

It took a couple of goes, but I managed to jump and grab a place where the soil wasn't too soft. I clambered up, threw myself over the side of the grave, and flopped onto my back. The corpses who'd been after me were nowhere to be seen. The skull lay right side up, that same creepy grin on its face. Or was it a snarl?

I rolled over and grimaced at my mud covered appearance. I grabbed the skull and a few of the other bones, tucked them under my arm, and headed back to Shamrock.

He was just where I'd left him, still breathing, but only just.

"I found something. I'm not sure they'll help us get out, but I think this is the source of the problems Silvaria's been having." I held out the skull.

Shamrock shrunk back and hid his eyes behind a hand.

"Yeah, that's the reaction I felt when I landed on the bones. I'll try it on the barrier and see if it has any impact." I jogged over and stuck the skull against the magic barrier.

The competing magic sparked together for a few seconds, but the barrier didn't lower.

"I guess you're no help to me." I tucked the skull back under my arm and returned to Shamrock. "We're going to have to wait this one out. Give me a few hours, and my magic should be up to defeating this barrier. Can you hold on that long?"

He shook his head.

"Of course you can. You're a rough, tough scarecrow. It'll take more than a little battering to defeat you."

He wheezed out what might have been a laugh, lifted his straw hand, and wiggled his fingers.

I grasped his hand, thinking he needed comfort, but the second I grabbed it, every muscle in my body tightened and the skull fell to the ground. My fingers clamped around his hand and I couldn't let go. A sweet smelling magic spun around me and the scent of warm, sun-drenched hay filled my nose.

I tried to speak, but my mouth wouldn't open, and my jaw locked.

My eyes widened. Shamrock was giving me his energy. I wriggled and squirmed, trying to break free, but I couldn't get away. He had to stop, or he'd die. Maybe he was just a scarecrow, but I was getting attached to this guy. He'd already saved me from some marauding corpses, and it looked like he was coming to my rescue again.

My frozen state didn't change for several minutes, as his sweet, warm magic twirled and danced around me. Finally, the smell of hay faded away, and my fingers unlocked.

I fell back, my body shaking and full of a strange magic that didn't feel at home inside a witch's body. "You didn't have to do that. I'd have found us a way out." My fingers and toes tingled, and sparks of bright orange flashed across my palms.

Shamrock gave a slight nod of his head. The light died in his eyes, and he heaved out a final sigh.

I dropped to my knees. "No! Don't go. I'll get help. You need to keep on breathing. Odessa will fix you, I know she will."

Shamrock lay there, nothing more than a damaged pumpkin with a straw body, dressed in oversized farm workers' clothes.

I touched his damaged pumpkin head. "I won't forget this sacrifice. Thank you."

I buzzed with energy, and it was an energy I'd struggle to control. It was bright and urgent and kept sparking out of me as if sensing it was in the wrong place.

I picked up the skull and yelped, sending it tumbling to the ground. My hands looked like they'd been burned from where I'd grabbed it.

"I guess you're not enjoying what's happening to you," I said. "But you're still coming with me. I need to figure out if you've messed with these corpses."

I took off my jacket, grabbed the skull and rolled it in it. I still felt the unpleasant magic seeping out, but at least it wasn't burning me.

The more exposure I had to this magic, the more it felt familiar. And it had a similar feel to the magic that had infected me when I was seventeen. This must be the work of the coven. The chaos in the cemetery was just another way they were messing with Witch Haven.

"You've failed this time," I muttered. "The corpses aren't going anywhere, and no one else is getting hurt."

I set down the skull in my jacket, and carefully moved my scarecrow friend to one corner of the cemetery, so he'd be out of the way and unnoticed. I didn't want to return and find he'd accidentally been put in the trash or recycled as pig feed.

I stroked Shamrock's cheek and gave it a quick kiss. "Just you wait, you'll be back to your old self in no time."

I collected the bones and headed to the magic barrier. I channeled some of the urgent, spiky scarecrow magic through my hands and leaned hard against it.

It took several minutes, and I was soon gasping for breath and shaking, but the barrier bent. I kept pushing, feeling like I was shoving through sticky tar, but suddenly I was free and out the other side of the barrier.

I heaved out a relieved sigh as I pushed open the gates. Getting through that barrier had drained me of nearly all of Shamrock's energy, but it had worked.

Now, I just needed to figure out what to do with these evil bones.

Chapter 14

I staggered up the porch steps of Magda's house. I stopped before opening the door. There was no way I was taking these creepy bones inside my house. I didn't want them messing with the chilled vibes.

I headed back down the steps and concealed the bones in a storage shed, before locking the door. Once my magic was recharged, I'd take a good hard look at them and see what I could find out.

Then I returned to the house and opened the door. I took a step inside and froze. Someone was moving about on the floor above me, and the noises being made were coming from something too big to be any of my familiars.

I poked my head into the living room. I'd already seen Russell sitting on the roof outside. Hilda was hanging from the huge web she'd been working on in the corner of the room, and Nugget was asleep on his pile of towels.

A floorboard above me creaked, and I tensed. Someone must have broken in.

I crept to the foot of the stairs, sparking what little magic I had left, and tilted my head, waiting to see what their next move would be. Was it a lurking corpse that had followed me from the cemetery? Or was something deadlier waiting for me?

There were several quiet footsteps along the corridor, heading away from the stairs. I narrowed my eyes and gritted my teeth as I crept closer. I was down to my last thread of patience. I'd been attacked by corpses, abandoned by Silvaria, fallen into a grave, and lost Shamrock. Whoever had decided to break into my house had picked the wrong day to mess with me.

I reached the top of the stairs and spotted someone scurrying away. I blasted out what was left of my magic. The person turned just before the spell hit them.

I gasped. It was Olympus. He staggered back as my magic slammed into him. Fortunately for him, I had barely any power left, so the only thing my spell damaged was the huge bouquet of roses he held.

"Olympus! What are you doing creeping around up here?" I stalked toward him.

"Waiting for you." His gaze was on the ruined bouquet.

"I thought you were an intruder. I could have killed you."

"Sorry. I didn't mean to startle you." He thrust out the charred flowers. "I got these for you. I'm so glad you're back. When you were taken, I thought the worst."

I ignored the burnt offering as my gaze ran over him. He was freshly shaven, smelled amazing, and wore a tuxedo with a perfectly tied black bowtie.

He stepped closer. "You are okay? I tried to find you, but you'd vanished. I looked everywhere."

"I'm fine. Silvaria and I had some business to take care of. I'm not understanding this, though." I gestured at his outfit. "Are you going to the opera or something?"

Olympus grinned. "This is for you. Do you like it?"

"Um... you really shouldn't have. I'm more of a faded jeans and leather jacket kind of woman. Although it's a step up from your Magic Council suits. They make you look uptight. And I'm glad you ditched the regulation work hat. No one can pull that off."

"Come with me, I have something to show you." Olympus grabbed my arm and yanked me into the main bedroom.

Uh, oh! It looked like Valentine's Day had snuck in and thrown up. The floor of my bedroom was covered in rose petals, scented candles burned on the dresser, and there was champagne on ice standing by the bed.

"I knew you'd come back to me," Olympus said.

"How did you know that? I could have been taken by the witch coven."

"You'd have defeated them, because you're an amazing witch. That's why I love you. And we're meant to be together. Nothing will keep us apart for long."

My cheeks heated. "Less of the love talk, or the intense let's be together forever stuff."

"Never. When I couldn't find you, I thought I'd do something fun for your return."

I glanced at him, wondering if this was a joke, but the look on his face was deadly serious.

"You can expect this every day when we're married. I wanted to give you a taste of things to come."

I squeezed my eyes shut for a second. "Olympus, we're not getting married, and you don't want to marry me."

He dropped to his knees and produced the ring again. "I do. And I'll keep asking until you say yes. I'm not giving up on us. And if the ring is the problem, I can change it. You can have whatever ring you like."

"There is no us. You have to stop doing these romantic gestures. It's weird."

He stood slowly and looked around. "Don't all women love flowers and to be romanced?"

I pursed my lips. "I don't love flowers. Once they're made into bouquets, they're basically dying or dead. They live a few days in water, but you're really only looking at rotting flowers in a vase. Get me a pot plant next time. Something hard to kill. A cactus would be good. I like those."

"Got it. No bouquets. Anything else?" His expression was so eager that I had to throw him a bone.

"I'm not a big drinker," I said. "Any more than two drinks, and I get a headache. I like hot chocolate, though."

"No champagne. Fine. How about the candles? Every woman likes scented candles."

I shook my head. "Unless I'm using them to cast a spell or center myself, scented candles give me a throbbing head. It's the smell, it's too overpowering."

His shoulders sagged. "I've done everything wrong. I tried to woo you and it failed. No wonder you won't accept my hand in marriage. I'm a terrible suitor."

I gave his arm a brief pat. "Don't worry about it. You're not yourself. And the Olympus I know would never do anything like this. You charm woman with your sarcasm. Although that's probably why you're still single."

"Huh? And you like that? You like me being mean to you?"

"Sarcasm's not about being mean to someone. It's funny."

"Then I shall be as horrible to you as I can." He pinched my arm. "How's that?"

I rubbed my arm and stepped back. "That's not sarcasm, that's domestic violence. Let's change the subject. I've had one heck of a day, and I need to relax."

Olympus clasped his hands together. "I know something you'd like."

"A sit down, a cup of coffee, and to be no longer troubled by dark magic?"

"No. This." He grabbed my face in his hands and planted a huge kiss on my lips.

I struggled in his grip and shoved him away. "Olympus! That's inappropriate. You'll regret doing that when you stop being such a weirdo."

"I thought you'd like it. You don't like kissing? Couples in love do that all the time."

"First off, we're not a couple. And second, we're not in love." I held up a hand to stop him protesting. "You're being messed with. Everyone who was in the cemetery the night we fought the corpses isn't behaving like themselves. And this isn't you. You don't want me."

A stubborn look crossed his face. "I do. And I want the real you, not this leather-clad minx you're hiding behind."

My eyebrows shot up. "You're the one who turned me into this leather-clad minx. You chose the crazy eyeliner, tight pants, and funky hair. You could have made me look like a sensible librarian when you picked the magic disguise."

"Let's remedy that." Olympus grabbed me again and kissed me. This time, the kiss had no hint of romance. It was full of magical intent, and that magic swirled through me, tingling my skin. The kiss swiftly grew intense as he held me against him.

I staggered back and gasped. That had been one heck of a magic-filled kiss. I'd felt it all the way down to my toes.

Olympus looked pleased with himself as he watched me sway. "How was that? Did you like that kiss?"

"That was..." I looked down at myself. I was back in my old clothes. I pulled a strand of hair in front of my face. My snarly dyed purple hair was also back. I dashed to the mirror. Yep, so was my old face. I was me again.

"Does that make you happy?" Olympus said.

I grinned at my reflection. "Yes! This is perfect."

"I know you don't believe me, but that's all I want to do. My purpose in life is to make you happy."

It was nice to hear someone say that, even though there was no truth behind those words. So, I simply nodded. There was no use fighting someone under a magical delusion. The more I fought Olympus, the more he'd dig in his heels and try to convince me it was all true.

It was time to play along. "Thanks, Olympus. The magic disguise was handy, but too many people have seen through it, Silvaria Digby included. And I feel better looking like myself."

"You really like it? You just ask, and I can change your appearance to whatever you want. Did you mention a librarian?" He lifted his hand.

"Nope. I'm good with being me."

Olympus walked over, and it looked like he was leaning in for another kiss.

Just for a second, I was tempted to let him lock lips with me again. That last kiss had been out of this world, but then it was full of magic, so the sparks should have flown.

I rested a hand on Olympus' chest and gently pushed him away. "We need less romance, and more action. I found something bad in the cemetery."

His forehead wrinkled, then he stepped back and nodded. "What can I do to help?"

"You can help, so long as you promise to keep those lips and those hands to yourself. And don't ask me to marry you again."

"Never?"

I hesitated. "Not for at least another ten years."

He pouted. "I guess I can wait. We can have a long engagement."

I huffed out a laugh. I had to give Olympus top marks for perseverance. "That's sounds great. Now, I need you to help me figure out how these clues fit together. You do still remember you work for the Magic Council?"

"Of course. I need a good job to keep you in the manner you're accustomed to." He glanced around my tired bedroom. "Or the manner we'll figure out together. One with newer furniture."

I shook my head. "Follow me." We needed to have this conversation on more neutral ground, where we weren't surrounded by romantic gestures that made me uncomfortable.

Olympus eagerly hurried down the stairs behind me and into the living room.

I settled on the couch, and he sat next to me, way too close. I shuffled to one side, making sure there was a respectable gap between us. "I think I found the source of the trouble in the cemetery. Someone dug a grave and placed a skeleton in it. I fell into the grave after being chased by corpses—"

"I should have been there to protect you. You shouldn't have to deal with corpses and skeletons on your own. I'm a terrible husband to-be."

I gritted my teeth and pressed on. "The second I moved the skull, the magic shifted. I think this skull holds a lot of power."

Olympus nodded, a fierce intensity on his face. "I'll destroy this skull for you. It would be my honor."

"Not yet. There's something I need to figure out about the skeleton in that grave. When I touched the bones, the magic felt familiar. I'm sure it's the same magic the witch coven used to bespell me and Magda all those years ago."

"I'm sure whatever you say is right. When would you like me to destroy the bones? I must make sure you're not at risk."

"Cool your heels. There won't be any destroying just yet. Not until I've run through a few spells to see if I can get any information out of them."

"That sounds dangerous. Let me do that."

I was tempted by the offer. Olympus was powerful, but he was also currently in the running for the title of King of the Weirdos. "No, you're good. And no offense, but while you're behaving so strangely, I don't trust your magic."

His bottom lip jutted out. "I'd never do anything to harm you. You can trust me."

"I hope that's true, but I don't want you accidentally blasting the bones apart and we lose an opportunity to see what they're hiding."

"Whatever you think best," he said. "You're always right."

I didn't like this docile, agreeable version of Olympus. I preferred it when he warned me I was overstepping the mark and being smart-mouthed. I needed someone to keep me in line at times. I'd quickly grow irritated with a guy who said yes to my every demand. There was no challenge in that.

"The skeleton isn't all I found. I also discovered some more of the black feathers that appeared after Luna's energy got taken, and the remains of my stolen ghost jar."

"A gothic wedding in autumn would be perfect for us," Olympus said.

I closed my eyes and massaged my forehead for a few seconds. "We're not talking about weddings. We're talking about cursed bones, toxic feathers, and a dangerous, escaped ghost."

"We could feature all of those in the wedding if you want them. You'd look beautiful in a black dress with a feather skirt."

"No, I'd look ridiculous." I flexed my hands, tempted to thump Olympus, but it wasn't his fault he was wedding obsessed. "I think these things are connected. Maybe the witches in the coven plan to use the corpses as their undead army. They're the frontline force to clear resistance, so it will be easy for them to make their final takeover bid on Witch Haven."

"And you should carry lilies. I've always thought lilies were beautiful."

"Lilies are for funerals. And you'll be going to your own funeral if you don't focus on what's important."

He ducked his head. "Our marriage is the most important thing to me. And it will be to you. I'll convince you an autumn wedding is what we need. Then you can stop worrying about strange bones, ghosts, and all that nastiness. You won't even need to work once you're my wife. You can be a stay at home witch."

"And go slowly insane while I bake arsenic muffins for you to enjoy and stick pins into your poppet?"

"No! You'll have no time for that. You'll be busy raising our children. I want at least six."

I rested my chin on my hands as I leaned forward and tried to shut out Olympus as he babbled about weddings, children, and the amazing life we'd have together. Maybe we would have a good life if we decided on trying out a real relationship, but there was no way I was going near this weird version of Olympus. All romance was off until my sharp, suspicious Olympus was back. Even then, I was undecided if I wanted anything from him. Relationships always got messy.

I looked at Nugget, who hadn't stirred the whole time I'd been in the house. Hilda was the same and only seemed focused on her web. Sadness shivered through me when I considered how much had changed so quickly. My familiars were now just your average house pets.

With their powers gone, my once useful asset and sort of friend in the Magic Council only interested in weddings and having babies with me, and my friends forgetting what powerful witches they were, I was in trouble.

"We need to fix the date so we can send out the invitations," Olympus said. "How about—"

I grabbed his head and planted a drugging kiss on his lips. Not in the hot and steamy drugging sense, but literally a drugging spell to send him into a deep sleep so he would stop talking.

Olympus groaned and slumped back.

I stood and lifted his legs so he was lying on the couch, then placed a cushion under his head.

"Sorry, but you're no good to me right now. Why don't you sleep off this strange magic? You'll be safe here. My—" I stopped and looked at my familiars.

They wouldn't be able to protect him. "You'll be safe. The house is warded."

I gave his cheek a soft pat. I expected a lot of women would give their right arm to be with an influential, powerful guy like Olympus. But I wasn't most women. I was a messed up witch, riding solo on a mission that was out of control. But I was done with feeling like that. It was time to grab back the reins and take command.

Chapter 15

The flickering light of the bonfire cast a welcome glow around my dark front yard.

I'd spent a couple of hours recharging my energy and not thinking about all the things I needed to tackle.

While I'd been recharging, Olympus hadn't stirred from the couch, and none of my familiars had paid me attention.

Now my magic was topped up, I was ready to deal with those bones and see what secrets they held.

I retrieved them from the storage shed and unwrapped them. Before I touched the bones, I dashed inside and grabbed some gloves, so I wouldn't get another painful sting. I also brought out the black feathers and the pieces of ghost jar.

I laid everything out in front of me, settled on an upturned log in front of the fire, and studied each item carefully. I started with what seemed to be the least dangerous item and inspected each piece of the broken ghost jar. Whoever had stolen the jar from my house must have been familiar with the ghost stuck inside it. But why would they want to free that ghost? It must be someone in alliance with the dark witches. Or was it one of the witches themselves? Had my house been invaded by the same dark energy that ripped my family apart all those years ago?

I glanced back at the house and shuddered. I hated the thought of my sanctuary being invaded. But it was possible that when I'd been racing around trying to find Luna, someone or something had snuck through my magic barrier. That seemed to be a reoccurring theme.

I turned my attention to the black feathers. They had a familiar, faint feel of magic to them, but I couldn't put my finger on where I'd felt it before. It was established magic and came from a magic user with power. Power that felt stable, as if they knew how to control it. Even though what remained on the feathers was weak, I could sense the strength behind the spell, and didn't like the possibility that I'd have to go up against this individual any time soon.

My gaze slid to the skull, and I frowned. "I don't know what you're smiling at? You're the source of the trouble in the cemetery." I nudged it with the toe of my boot.

It continued to grin.

I made sure my gloves were on tight and then lifted the skull. I grimaced as the unpleasant magic wriggled against me. It was so tempting to toss the skull into the fire or shatter it with a hammer. Every nerve warned me to step away from this power, and that no good would come from being so close to such darkness.

But I couldn't get the wobbles now. I sucked in a breath and cast a reveal spell over the skull.

My magic swirled around it, bouncing against it as if meeting an invisible resistance.

"Come on, stop hiding. Or are you scared to show me your true face?"

My spell couldn't get through, no matter how hard I focused.

"You're scared of me," I whispered. "You wouldn't be going all cloak and dagger if you thought you were invulnerable. Well, you're not. You're just a bully, and no one likes bullies."

I set the skull down with the rest of the bones and cast a spell over them to remove the magic barrier. There was something lurking beneath the surface, but it didn't want to give up its secrets, and the spell slid off the bones.

"If you were created by the witch coven, why don't you take me over like the last time? You can use me just like those corpses you've been having fun with."

The skull wobbled from side to side, as if considering this possibility.

"That's got you thinking. I bet you wouldn't mind an Ash witch on your side. We're powerful, in case you didn't know. And I'm the last in line, so dragging me back to the dark side would be an added bonus."

The skull stopped moving. I cast a few more spells, but nothing had any effect.

It was getting late, but I couldn't give up yet. I grabbed a bag, gathered up the bones, feathers, and the ghost jar, and placed them inside. I shrugged on my jacket, doused the bonfire, and made sure I had my hat pulled down over my face so no one would recognize me, then headed into the village.

There was someone I'd been meaning to talk to. It was time to confront Albert and see if his Mr. Nice Guy act was just that. I wasn't convincing myself that he was a dark overlord come to wreak havoc on sleepy little Witch Haven, but he was always around when trouble stirred. I had to see if there was anything behind that.

The bakery was closed when I got there, but Albert lived in the apartment upstairs. I rang the bell and waited.

A moment later, a light came on in the bakery, and Albert headed to the door. He smiled brightly when he saw me and gave me a cheery wave. What did he have to be so happy about? His plan to take his niece's energy had failed.

He threw the door open wide. "Indigo! It feels like I haven't seen you in forever. Have you been avoiding me?"

I narrowed my eyes. "Not really. But it's been a busy few weeks."

"I'll say it has. I've just had a huge order for a wedding party. I'm not sure how I'll find the time to bake everything. You must come in and fill me in on your news."

I glanced behind me, checking Albert wasn't trying to dupe me, but there was no group of angry villagers about to pounce. I walked into the bakery and waited for him to close the door.

"Would you like a cake? Everything is packed away in the fridges, but I can get you something.

How about a salted caramel muffin? Or a blueberry tart?"

I shook my head. Albert had fooled me once with his delicious cakes, I wasn't going there again. "I'm not here for your food."

"Are you sure? I can even make you something fresh."

"No, I'm here about Luna and what happened in the cemetery."

"Oh, you mean her send-off? Wasn't it wonderful? I'm so glad I made the effort to do it. People said I was being foolish, but it's important to have closure."

"Is that what you call it? I heard it didn't exactly go to plan."

He gestured at a table and settled in a seat. I joined him and perched on the edge of the seat opposite him. I placed the bag with my dark magic goodies beside me.

"I'd have liked more people to be there, but those that mattered got to say goodbye to Luna," he said.

"Albert, you weren't saying goodbye to her. You were taking her energy. You don't even know for certain she's dead. And you must know what happens if you tear magic from someone who is still alive."

He shuddered. "You're mistaken. I'd never do that. This was just a final farewell. And it's nice that I have somewhere I can go when I want to talk to Luna. I don't have much family left because..." he waved a hand at me. "Well, I don't need to explain that to you. Luna was happy to put up with the prattlings of an old man. She was such a kind child. Well, young woman. You've all grown up so fast."

"Luna was amazing. And she still is, but I think she's in trouble because of the darkness in the village."

"Darkness? I'm not sure I understand."

"Neither do I. Not completely." I rested a hand on the bag. "I've got some things to show you, and I need you to be honest with me about them." This could get bad really quickly if these items triggered Albert's dark side. That's even if he had one, but I had to know for sure if he was involved.

His eyebrows raised, but he nodded.

I set out the pieces of ghost jar, the feathers, and then the skull.

He grimaced as he looked at the items. "Where did you get those?"

"The skull came from a grave in the cemetery. The rest of the items I found lying around in the same place."

His head jerked back. "You dug up a grave to take that skull?"

"No, this one was open. And, in case you've forgotten all the fun you had in the cemetery, the dead are rising. It would be easy to grab dozens of bones from the wandering corpses."

"Wandering... corpses?" He scratched the side of his head. "I don't know anything about that."

That made no sense. Albert remembered going to the cemetery, but not being attacked by the corpses. Was that because his magic was involved? "Are you also claiming not to know anything about these things?"

"I... no! Why should I?"

"You know nothing about cursed bones that make the dead rise and magic fade?"

Albert's mouth opened and closed several times. "I'm at a loss to know what to tell you. I have nothing to do with curses. My magic focuses on positivity. Spells and sugar, that's my speciality. Besides, why would I want to curse anyone?"

"That's what I'm here to find out. Touch the skull."

He shook his head. "No. I don't like the feel of it. And it's not natural to carry that around. If you believe it's dangerous, you should destroy it, or hand it to the Magic Council."

"I need to know if you're familiar with the spells on it. Touch the skull. If it's your magic, it'll recognize you."

"I won't! It could be tainted. Put it away." His body shuddered, and he wrapped his arms around himself, as if seeking comfort.

My gut told me Albert was the least likely person to ever use dark magic, but he'd been involved with this mystery from the beginning. His niece had disappeared, he'd drugged me and my friends and almost burned us at the stake, and he had been in the cemetery, casting magic to get his hands on more power. Had I been duped by this nice, easy to forget guy?

"I was thinking about your relationship with your late wife," I said.

His expression turned puzzled. "What about it? I'm surprised you even remember her."

"I remember everyone who died the day me and Magda attacked the village. You didn't have a good relationship, did you?"

He stared at me. "We were a married couple. We had a few issues, but we got along just fine. Why? What are you suggesting?"

"What did you do after she died? Did you take her magic, just like you planned to do with Luna's?"

Albert did an impressive goldfish impression for several seconds. "Well, since you mention it, I did take my wife's power. She also specialized in food magic, and I saw no harm in taking it. Having my wife's energy enhances what I can do for the bakery. And she wouldn't have minded. She loved this place."

"You had an agreement? You both agreed that if one of you died, the other could have their energy?"

Albert gulped. "Not in so many words. It was more of an unwritten understanding. It was logical that I take it."

It may have been logical, but it was also illegal. A magic user must agree in front of two witnesses to have their energy transferred to someone else upon their death.

"Indigo, I don't like where you're going with this questioning," Albert said. "And I really don't like the fact you've brought these tainted magic objects into my bakery. I shall have to have it cleansed."

I wasn't apologizing for questioning a suspect in this mystery. "You do that. But I'm not going to stop asking questions until Luna is safely back with us. Or don't you want me to keep looking for her?"

Albert pushed back his chair. "I suggest you leave. I have nothing to tell you about curses or corpses, and it's upsetting that you're suggesting I don't care about Luna. I was feeling good about saying goodbye to her, and now you've ruined everything."

I remained in my seat. "I've had a doozy of a time recently, and I had a feeling you were behind it."

His chin wobbled, but he glared at me. "You're wrong. I know nothing about these feathers, walking corpses, or any of the other oddities you've talked about. Now, if you don't mind, I was about to go to bed."

I collected up the items and followed Albert to the bakery door. I walked out and then turned. "Albert. Catch!" I threw the skull at him.

On reflex, he reached out and grabbed it. He was blasted across the bakery and hit the back wall. He slid down it and groaned. The skull slipped from his fingers and rolled away.

I raced over to him and checked for a pulse. I blew out a breath when I discovered he was alive.

"What happened?" He groaned. "Something hit me. It felt like a sledgehammer."

"Holy broomsticks! Albert, I'm sorry. I had to see if the skull magic was connected to you, and you wouldn't touch the skull, so I figured I'd make you. I had no idea it would do that to you." I eased him forward and checked the back of his head. There was a cut, and a large lump was forming.

"Skull magic?" He moaned and leaned forward. "I don't feel too good. What's going on?"

"I made a mistake. If that had been your magic, it wouldn't have reacted to you like that. I'm really sorry." I stayed beside him as he huffed and puffed and complained about a headache. "Can you stand? You'll feel better once you're on your feet."

It took a few minutes of persuading, but I got Albert into a chair. I rushed into the kitchen, grabbed a bag of ice, and headed back into the bakery. I rested the ice against his lump and glanced at the skull. It was definitely smirking at me.

"I'm having some odd memories," Albert said. "Do you think I have a concussion?"

"Most likely. You blasted across the room like a jet-propelled bat. We'll let the swelling go down, and then I'll do some healing magic on you. You'll feel better after that."

He glanced at me. "Thank you. Although why did you do that? Don't you trust me?"

I was ashamed of my actions, and it had been a desperate move to try to find answers. A move that had badly backfired. "I wasn't thinking straight. And all the mysteries in Witch Haven are driving me crazy."

Albert closed his eyes. "What you were saying to me... I'm remembering being in the cemetery, and there were corpses everywhere. I asked other people to help me. I did want Luna's energy. But that can't be right. I'd never take her power from her. I don't even know she's dead."

I crouched beside him and clasped his hand. Maybe this bump on the head was a good thing. "Albert, that's right. You're remembering what really happened to Luna."

He blinked rapidly at me. "Yes! At least, I think I am. I remember her being in the hospital and she was sick. And then she was recovering, but was taken. Luna vanished. And you were helping to look for her. You haven't found her, have you?"

I clutched his hand. "Not yet. But I'm not giving up on her, and neither should you."

"I'll never give up on Luna." He shook his head and winced. "What was I thinking, performing a ceremony to take her magic? And why am I only just remembering this?"

"It's not your fault. There's strange magic going around that's making people act oddly, and that includes memory loss. I think it's linked to the cemetery, and probably that skull you touched."

He looked at the skull and shuddered. "There's something very wrong with that. The second I caught it, pain slammed through me."

"It doesn't want to give up any secrets." I let go of his hand, removed the ice, and then pressed my palm against the lump on his head. "I'll do some healing spells to make you feel better."

He nodded, then sat quietly as I performed my magic.

I felt terrible for what I'd done to Albert. I hadn't been convinced he was the mastermind behind this darkness, but I was desperate to know the truth. And he hadn't wanted to touch the skull. He'd seemed guilty.

But I was an idiot, and I'd been wrong. Albert was just as confused and bespelled as everyone else.

It took a good half an hour of intensive healing before the lump on his head went down. Once again, my magic was drained, and I felt almost too weary to move by the time I stepped away from Albert.

"I feel so much better," he said. "And I really am sorry I can't help you figure out what's going on with that skull."

"Don't apologize. I should never have brought it to you."

"Can you get it out of here? I don't want it putting off the customers, and I'm hoping its dark energy doesn't linger."

"Of course. I won't bother you again. And I really am sorry. I just... well, I messed up."

"It seems I've been making a few mistakes around here too. I'm... well, I'm not sure how to say this." He smoothed a hand over his receding hair. "I remember drugging you and your friends and trying to have you burned at the stake. Is that true?"

I patted his shoulder. "It is true, but you weren't yourself. And as you can see, I'm still here. I wasn't even a tiny bit charred."

"I shouldn't have done that. I'm not feeling myself. I get so angry, and want to... I'm ashamed to say, I want to hurt people."

"You're not alone. And I'm hoping I can fix that."

Albert was quiet for a few seconds. "How about we draw a line under all of this and start again? I don't mean you any ill will. And you were a good friend to Luna."

"I'm still a good friend to her. Don't go giving up on her." I grabbed the skull and placed it back in the bag. "I'll get out of your way."

"Yes. And I'll go to bed. I have a lot to think about."

"We all do. Good night, Albert."

"Good night. And, Indigo, you will help Luna, won't you?"

The sadness and confusion on his face had me instantly nodding. "Of course. I'm not giving up on her until I know the truth."

His smile was sad as he showed me out of the store, then closed the door behind me.

I walked away, my head down as I stuck to the shadows. That had been a total bust.

I needed a new lead to follow. I also needed allies on my side, but I wasn't sure where to turn to find any. Everyone I cared about had either lost their memory or was being too weird to trust.

After casting so much magic again, I was exhausted. Much like Albert, I needed rest, a clear head, and then to make a new plan of action.

Chapter 16

Dawn was breaking through the window as I rolled out of bed the next morning. I stretched and flexed my fingers. I felt so much better after grabbing some sleep, and my magic no longer felt like it was about to spiral out of me and slide down the drain like soiled water.

I crept down the stairs after showering and dressing and checked on Olympus. He was stirring on the couch, but his eyes were still closed.

I headed into the kitchen, brewed coffee and filled a thermos with it, then took out two tins of my favorite peaches and placed them in my bag, along with the skull, feathers, and ghost jar fragments.

Then I made a mug of coffee and headed into the living room, planning to leave it for Olympus so he'd find it when he woke.

He was sitting up, looking bleary-eyed. His hair was adorably sleep ruffled and stubble dusted his usually clean-shaven chin.

"Hey! I didn't mean to wake you. It's still early. Go back to sleep," I said.

His face brightened when he saw me. "You're such an angel, looking after me so well. I don't know what happened last night. I didn't mean to fall asleep on you. I didn't do anything inappropriate, did I?"

I repressed a grin. "Don't worry about it. Drink this." I handed him the coffee.

"Where's yours? Aren't you going to stay with me? We have so many plans to discuss."

I backed away to the door. "No time. We have a whole village to save, remember?"

"Five minutes. We can talk about wedding themes." Olympus went to set his mug down on top of the pile of Magda's journals.

I grabbed the mug and set it on the table. "Don't get a coffee ring on those."

He rubbed his eyes and yawned. "What are they?"

"Evidence. Although I'm not so sure they're that useful. I keep reading through those journals, expecting them to give me more guidance, but nothing has shown up. Maybe Magda really knew nothing else about the coven."

Olympus leaned forward and lifted one off the pile. He opened it and flicked through it. "It's a shame Magda can't be at our wedding."

"No one's going to be at our wedding."

He glanced at me. "You're still thinking about my proposal, though? Am I still in with a chance of winning your hand?"

I walked over and sat next to him. "Think about something else. Anything. Don't you have things to do for the Magic Council?"

"I will need to book time off for our honeymoon. Do you like warm sandy beaches, or are you more into exploring?"

I shook my head. Olympus had his bedazzled heart set on marrying me, and nothing else seemed to matter. "I'll let you know."

He grinned and nodded enthusiastically before returning his attention to the journal. He traced a finger down the page he was looking at. "Magda wrote some odd things in here. This whole page is devoted to being careful around loved ones."

I slid him a glance. She'd got that right. At the moment, I couldn't depend on anyone I cared about. "What else did she say?"

"It doesn't make sense to me. Magda repeated several times that you shouldn't always trust loved ones. Aren't they the people you should trust the most? I trust you with my life."

"Maybe hold off on being too trusting around me," I said.

"I'd never doubt you. You're the perfect woman for me." Olympus set down the journal. "And Magda didn't get everything right." He gave me a meaningful look.

Olympus may not think Magda was such a wise woman, but she'd raised me well, and I knew when to pay attention when she dispensed words of wisdom.

"Will you invite any family to our wedding?" Olympus said.

"Nope. There's no one to invite."

"You don't have any living relatives left?"

"Not a single one."

He took hold of my hand and kissed the back of it. "I've got plenty of family. And your friends will come, won't they?"

I sighed. "I reckon they will."

His warm smile tempted me to play along, and just for a few minutes, think about planning a wedding with a cute guy. I'd definitely take wedding stress over corpse wandering stress and missing friend stress any day. But I didn't have time to indulge in fantasies.

"Olympus, close your eyes. I've got a surprise for you."

He gave my hand a squeeze, and then obediently closed his eyes. I didn't like to keep drugging him with magic, but it was better if he stayed out of the way. If he wandered into this big mess when he wasn't himself, he could get killed.

I leaned in and gave him a kiss which sent him slumping back on the couch. I made sure he was comfortable, there was food down for my familiars, or should I say, my pets, and then left the house.

Olympus could fix himself food when he woke up, which wouldn't be for several hours. And that gave me time to tackle my next task.

I needed an ally. Although the potential ally I had in mind had badly let me down the last time we worked together, but I didn't know who else to turn to. And Silvaria Digby owed me after abandoning me to the marauding corpses.

I walked to the cemetery. The early hour meant there was no-one around to point the finger and yell at me, but I still hurried along and kept my head down to avoid being noticed.

I entered through the cemetery gates easily. The magic barrier Silvaria had put in place was gone.

Inside, it looked pristine and untouched. You'd never have known that just yesterday there were gangs of overexcited corpses bounding around.

I did a quick check of my deceased scarecrow friend and was pleased to see Shamrock hadn't been moved. I gave his head a quick pat and then left him alone. I'd be back for him as soon as I had a spare moment, and once Odessa was her old self and could repair him.

It took me about twenty minutes to walk around the cemetery, looking for Silvaria. She wasn't the easiest cemetery guardian to find. Anyone would think she didn't like hanging out with the living.

I'd done two circuits and was getting irritated when I heard footsteps marching toward me. I turned to see Silvaria stomping over, bone stick in her hand.

"I see you're not wearing that ridiculous ghost hunter hooker disguise anymore."

"It's nice to see you, too," I said.

"How are you not dead?"

"It's no thanks to you. You abandoned me in the middle of the corpse apocalypse."

She huffed out a breath. "It's survival of the fittest in this place. It's a rule I've lived by for years. It works."

I looked around. "You have little competition here when it comes to survival rates."

Silvaria scowled at me. "So, what happened? Did my residents decide you weren't tasty enough to eat?"

I wasn't revealing my scarecrow helper to Silvaria. "You left your barrier in place. I could have been trapped in here."

"That's the whole point of a barrier. It keeps things in, and unwanted things from creeping out."

"I'm hardly an unwanted thing." I yanked back my anger before I said something I'd regret and ruin the one chance I had of finding an ally. "Silvaria, I'm not here to argue. I'm here to call in a favor."

"I don't owe you anything."

"Not true." I raised my eyebrows and glared at her.

She rolled her eyes. "Fine, maybe I panicked. But those corpses wouldn't stop coming, and since I figured you were messed up in getting them all twitchy, I decided to leave you to it."

I pulled out the thermos of coffee and tinned peaches. "I haven't had breakfast yet. Do you want to join me?"

Silvaria sucked in air through her teeth as she studied my offerings. "It's not the worst idea I've ever heard. Follow me." She walked to the back of the cemetery where there was a small, tumbledown looking storage shed. She pushed open the door and walked in.

The inside didn't match the exterior. It was almost cozy, with a large armchair in one corner, throw cushions scattered around, and a small heater that lifted the chill from the worn wooden frame.

Silvaria dropped into the seat. "You'll have to sit on the floor. I don't have visitors often, so I'm not set up for company."

"No problem." I poured the coffee, then opened the tinned peaches. I handed her a tin.

She wrinkled her nose, but took it. "So, what do you want from me?"

I took a sip of my coffee. "I'm trying to understand you."

Silvaria snorted a laugh. "You want to play head shrink?"

"No, but you act like you don't care about anything, and you said you wanted to give up and let the corpses take you."

"I wasn't lying. It would have been an easy out."

I nodded. "But then you vanished."

"And..."

"And I think you aren't as cynical as you make out. You want to be a part of this community just as badly as I do. And you don't want Witch Haven to be wiped off the map."

She waved a hand in front of her face. "My escaping had nothing to do with wanting to be a pillar of the community."

"So why flee when you had a chance to end it all?"

Silvaria gulped down several peaches. "I don't like leaving a mess behind. If the corpses had gotten me, there'd be no one to clean up the cemetery. I haven't been to bed yet because I've been working on putting everything right."

Silvaria cared, she just didn't like to admit it. And that meant she might agree to help me. "You did an amazing job. I hardly recognized the place when I arrived."

Her scowl softened. "I take pride in my work. Besides, no one would do half as good a job as me.

If I'd been dragged away by those corpses, Witch Haven cemetery would be in ruins. I didn't want that on my conscience."

"But you didn't mind leaving me behind?"

"Don't take it personally, but I don't like the living. They talk too much, and they're always asking for things." She lifted one shoulder. "And I had a feeling you'd be able to handle yourself. And you did, since you're here, talking to me. Talking a lot, I might add. I'll get one of my headaches if I'm not careful."

I ate a slice of peach. Despite her surly manner, Silvaria hadn't given up on life. "Now I know you do care about this place, I need your help with a puzzle."

She lifted her chin, but didn't speak.

I finished my coffee and opened the bag I'd brought with me. "I found some weird things in the cemetery. Things I can't explain. Maybe you'll know how they're all connected." I lifted out the pieces of ghost jar, the feathers, and the skull.

"I found some of those feathers when I was tidying up," Silvaria said. "I didn't like the feel of them. And when I burned them, they fizzled."

"They're connected to whatever took Luna's energy. The magic in them is weak, but it doesn't feel positive. The same goes for the skull, although that's bubbling with something nasty. I found it in an open grave that was tucked away in the trees."

Silvaria's gaze lifted to the door. "That can't be right. There are no grave sites among the trees. I'm not permitted to dig there because it makes the roots unstable."

"Someone did. That's where I found the skeleton. And I believe the magic contained within the bones is dark enough and powerful enough to stir up everyone here."

Silvaria slurped up the last of her peaches and thumped down the tin. She stared at the skull in silence for a minute. "So that's the source of my problems?"

"I think so. Have you had any more wandering corpses since I took this away?" I said.

"No, not that there were that many left. I can't believe one small witch did so much damage."

"I'm more powerful than I look."

"What's with those pottery fragments?"

"They belong to a ghost jar. I captured a spirit in it. The jar was taken from my house, and I found it smashed in the cemetery. You need to keep an eye out for a malevolent spirit. If it's hanging around your graves, it'll only cause problems."

"It's an interesting mix you've brought me." A gleam of interest lit Silvaria's eyes as she leaned closer. She touched the feathers, then the pieces of ghost jar. "I'm not getting much off those. I know grave magic, and it's not emanating from these items. These weren't used to wake my dead."

"What about the skull? Be careful if you handle it. It's given me a nasty jolt."

Silvaria touched the skull. She drew back slowly and rubbed the tip of her finger.

"Did you feel something?"

She looked at me and her eyes narrowed. "I'm not sure. Is this a test?"

"No, I really need your help. What did you sense?"

Silvaria made a grab for the skull, but I caught her hand. "Careful! This skull blasted Albert Black across his bakery when he touched it."

"What's Albert got to do with this?"

I grimaced. "It's a long story. Just go easy with the skull. If it can make an entire cemetery of dead people get up and walk, it's got power."

Silvaria touched the feathers again and then turned her attention back to the skull. She placed her palms on top of it and closed her eyes.

I chewed on my bottom lip as I waited to see what would happen. Her forehead was scrunched in concentration and her eyes squeezed tight shut.

When she looked at me, anger burned in her gaze. "Is this a joke?"

"I'm deadly serious. What did you feel?"

Silvaria leaned back as far as she could, as if she didn't want to be anywhere near me. "You need to leave. And take those cursed items with you."

"Silvaria, wait! I don't get it. What did you feel when you touched the skull?"

She reared up out of her seat, snatched up the items and stuffed them in the bag, which she thrust in my hands. "Go!"

I stood firm. "Not until you tell me what you got off that skull. Do you know who infused it with magic?"

Silvaria growled at me, then shoved me toward the door. "I should have paid attention to the gossip, but I never like it when people talk badly of others. I've had enough of that myself to last a lifetime."

"What do you mean? Gossip about me?"

"I was an idiot. Everything I've heard about you is true." She shoved me out the door so hard, I almost lost my balance and hit the dirt.

Whatever she'd felt in that skull had made her angry, but it was more than that. When I looked closely, there was fear flickering in Silvaria's eyes.

"I have no idea what you're talking about."

"Of course you do. You must be able to feel it." She pointed at the bag.

"Feel what?"

Silvaria shook her head as she backed away. "The magic in that skull. It belongs to you."

Chapter 17

I stared at Silvaria, my mouth open. I was so shocked my whole body shuddered. "The magic in the skull has nothing to do with me."

"I know Ash witch magic when I feel it, and it's buried deep in that skull. I don't know what you expected me to do. Were you hoping I wouldn't be able to detect it?"

"No! Because there's nothing to detect. Not from me, anyway."

"What did you plan to do next? Place the skull in the village water supply so it infected everyone with your darkness?"

"I'd never do that. I'm trying to help."

"You used me to make sure nothing could be traced back to you. If I couldn't sense your power in that skull, no one would be able to. You'd have gotten away with it."

I shook my head. "You're wrong. Touch the skull again. You'll realize the magic isn't mine." I went to grab the skull from the bag, but Silvaria hissed at me.

"Keep your toxic magic away from me. And get out of my cemetery. You've been behind everything that's gone wrong in this village all this time. You came back here to have another go at taking control and ruining people's lives. You won't succeed. We're on to you this time."

I staggered back as if she'd punched me. "That's not true. I... I just want a quiet life."

"A quiet life," she said in a mocking tone. "I hate being deceived. I almost trusted you and thought you were trying to do the right thing. I'm reporting this to the Magic Council. And you'll have nowhere to hide now. They'll know you're here, and without your disguise, they'll arrest you."

I took a step back and sucked in a breath. "Silvaria, you have to believe me. I—"

"No, I don't. You'd better start running. You've messed with my cemetery for the last time." She slammed the door in my face.

I stared at the closed door, my heart pounding so hard I thought it might burst out of my chest. I couldn't be involved with this. This magic wasn't mine, was it?

I dumped the contents of the bag on the ground and stared at the skull. "What did you do to Silvaria? Why did you make her think my magic is involved with this darkness?"

As usual, the skull didn't speak.

My throat was tight and my vision hazed. Was I involved with this and didn't realize? Other villagers were struggling with memory loss, and it wouldn't be the first time dark magic had used me. Was this whole thing a setup? I'd been guided back here by the very darkness I'd been trying to escape from since I was a teenager.

Had it brought me back after Magda died, and lured me in with the promise of home, friends, and familiars? It made me care about things, and all this time, it was using me to put the final nail in the coffin for Witch Haven.

I gritted my teeth, my hands clenched as my breath rasped out of me. Everything I loved was slipping through my fingers. And now this. I was so done with being messed around.

I jabbed a finger at the skull. "This is your fault." I raised my foot and brought my heel down on the middle of the skull.

It rolled away, completely unharmed. A curl of black smoke rose from the mouth of the skull. The smoke drifted to about the height of my waist and then faded on the breeze.

"That's it? That's all you've got? Why aren't you conjuring up werewolves or vampires to take me out? You're not so strong now I know what you're playing at." I whirled around as a low, pained groan reached my ears.

The light dimmed in the cemetery as black clouds poured across the sky and lightning flickered around me.

I gulped. Maybe I'd spoken too soon.

There was a shuffling, scratching noise coming from all around me. I hurried toward the graves to see hands poking out of the mud. Oh, crud. Rather than destroying the magic in that skull, I'd simply triggered it and woken the cemetery residents again.

The door to Silvaria's shed slammed open. She raced out, a shovel in her hands. She looked around, her eyes wide. "You're unbelievable! I've just got everyone settled."

"This has nothing to do with me. I mean, I did kick the skull, so it's not happy with me. It's the skull doing this."

"Why did you kick it if you knew it would aggravate the dead?"

"I didn't know this would happen. I wanted to destroy it, but it wouldn't break." I looked around as the corpses slowly rose. "I think I unleashed something."

"You unleashed your evil magic into my corpses." Silvaria swung the shovel at me. "If I had any doubts you were behind this, I have none now. Get out of here before you release even more problems."

I grabbed the skull and backed away. I slammed into a corpse, and it wrapped its bony arms around me and squeezed.

I squeaked and wriggled out of its grip, before charging away. I didn't get far before I hit a wall of angry corpses.

"Get her!" Silvaria yelled. "She's the one disturbing your slumber. Kill the witch!"

Why did people keep yelling that at me? I wasn't a bad witch. Not deliberately.

I dodged around another corpse and headed to the gate, but I was too slow, and the way out was blocked by swaying, moaning bodies.

What I wouldn't give to have a fang wielding spider, an awesome crow, and a snarky cat by my side to take this lot out.

I blasted some of the corpses out of my way, but more filled the gap. I slowed as I got nearer the gate. The corpse blockade was too dense to get through.

I turned, almost running straight into another corpse. I dodged around it and bolted across the cemetery. There had to be another way out.

I made it part of the way around the perimeter, before I realized I was being followed.

The corpses I'd awakened looked intent on murder as they loped after me, body parts going flying as they picked up speed.

I blasted a few more away and spotted a large crypt that I hoped was empty. I tugged open the heavy stone door, looked inside, and breathed out a sigh of relief. No one was home. They were probably already shambling around the cemetery.

I shut the door behind me and leaned on it as I got my breath back.

I dropped the skull and kicked it away. I was still reeling over Silvaria's revelation. She couldn't be right. Ash witch magic wasn't behind this.

Ash witches were good witches. My line of magic users was known for standing up for the weak and making sure justice was served. We weren't vengeful witches, and we always made sure the bad guys got what they deserved.

And it was only me left. Unless I'd been given a complete memory wipe and dark magic controlled me, I hadn't done this to the bones. I wasn't the one who'd cursed the corpses and made them rise. But if this magic was from the Ash witch line, it had to be me. There was no one else who could have done it.

I cautiously picked up the skull and placed it on top of the tomb in the center of the crypt. I had to know the truth. Was my magic causing all this trouble?

I stroked my hands across the amethyst necklace I wore, thinking about Magda, her warm, comforting power, and everything she'd done that was good in this world.

The necklace warmed reassuringly beneath my fingers.

I settled my panicked mind and focused on the skull. "You will reveal your secrets to me." I held my hands over it and let my magic pulse out in a solid wave.

Nothing happened. The skull didn't wobble or smoke. It remained still.

I took a couple of deep breaths, rolled my shoulders, and tried again. This time, I removed my gloves and pressed both hands on either side of the skull. My skin sizzled, but I kept my hands clamped around it.

"Reveal yourself."

The skull shook.

"Give up your secrets. Who is behind this corpse trouble?" I blasted more magic into the skull, the necklace growing uncomfortably warm against my skin.

It wobbled and bucked beneath my hand and then shot off the tomb. I ducked as it whizzed around like an out-of-control broomstick.

The skull stopped in the middle of the crypt, hovering several feet off the ground. Then it began to spin and hum, getting so fast it was just a blur.

The air heated and my ears popped.

It was like a bomb blast went off. The door blew off the crypt as a flare of magic shot out of the skull and swept across the cemetery and beyond the wall.

I glanced around, and my eyes widened. "I don't believe it. How did you survive that?"

The skull was still in one piece on the ground.

Something brushed against my collarbone, and I looked down to see my necklace had been destroyed.

"No!" My heart froze for a second. I needed that necklace. It helped me to control my magic and become strong again. Without it, I was the same failed witch I'd been when I'd returned to Witch Haven.

I dropped to my knees and pressed my head against the side of the tomb. I wanted to give up. My magic was weak, the skull was taunting me, and the corpses were coming for me. Everything I tried to do to stop this dark magic had the opposite effect. And I had no clue what I'd just unleashed on the village, but the spell that had shot out of the skull had power behind it.

I jerked my head up and jumped to my feet. The sound of groaning corpses outside was getting nearer, but that wasn't all I could hear. The lid on the tomb was opening.

I instinctively reached for my necklace, but I had nothing to fall back on.

Silvaria appeared in the doorway of the crypt. Her chest was heaving and mud was smeared down one side of her face. "What did you do?"

I puffed out a sigh. "The skull sent out a magic blast."

"No kidding. All my dead are rising, and they're raging mad. They want blood." She lifted an injured hand to me.

I glanced at the lid of the crypt as it continued to slide open. "It's not safe to stay in here."

"And it's dangerous out there." Silvaria shot a thumb over her shoulder. "Nowhere is safe, thanks to you."

"Let's get out in the open. I don't want to be trapped in here with whatever's coming out of this tomb."

Silvaria grimaced at the sound of stone grinding together. "You're right there. The magic user inside that tomb won't be happy he's been woken after three hundred years on his back."

I grabbed the skull and hurried out with Silvaria.

The corpses were wandering around, not looking happy. Several of them turned in our direction, but they weren't what caught my attention. I grabbed Silvaria's arm.

She shook me off and tutted. "Stay away from me. I don't want to be polluted by your magic."

I pointed at the cemetery gates. "You don't have to worry about me. It's them you have to be concerned about."

Coming through the gates were a horde of angry villagers, and they were heading straight for me.

"Oh, no! This mess has nothing to do with me. I won't be held responsible for this." Silvaria backed away. "You caused this chaos, you have to pay for what you've done."

"Silvaria! Don't you dare. You can't leave me again," I said.

"Sorry, witch. It's every cemetery guardian for herself. You're on your own." Silvaria clicked her fingers and disappeared.

I glanced around, looking for an escape route, but there was nowhere to go. I had corpses at my back and villagers at my front. And it looked like the whole village had descended upon the cemetery, and they all had evil intent in their eyes as they raced toward me.

Among the crowd, I spotted Odessa and Storm. I raised a hand to wave them over, but then lowered it. They were yelling and seemed as angry as everyone else.

A blur of blackness shot past my head, and I ducked. It was Russell, and he was attacking me.

This was too much. My friends and familiars now wanted me dead.

"Grab the witch," someone yelled. "Don't let her get away."

No one was grabbing me. I was done with being drugged, yelled at, almost flambéed, and accused of things I hadn't done.

My friends may have given up on me, but I wasn't giving up on them. I just needed more power so I could destroy the source of this darkness.

I ran toward Odessa and Storm, knocking other villagers out of the way, and blasting any with magic that got too close and threatened me.

Although the villagers were all angry, there was also a heady mix of fear in the group. No one wanted to be the first to attack me, but once the spells started flying, I was done for.

I was glad no one wanted to make the first move. It bought me a little time. Time to try something I had no idea would work.

Storm snarled as she got closer. Odessa was right beside her, and I was shocked to see the furious expression on her face. Odessa didn't do angry.

"Come and get me," I yelled at them. I had to believe that whatever spell had them in its thrall, my real friends were still in there, and they'd be able to help me.

I dodged past several villagers and led Storm and Odessa away from the largest group. Once we were out of striking distance of any other villager or corpse, I turned and stopped, waiting until we were face-to-face.

"Stop running from us!" Odessa panted out. "You have to pay."

"I'm paying for nothing. I know you hate me right now, and just like everyone else, you want me dead. But I need you to do one thing for me. Call it a last request."

"All you need to do is die," Odessa said.

Storm nodded and cracked her knuckles.

"And if this doesn't work, then I will be dead. I promise, I won't fight you if you want to kill me. I'll stand here and take it."

They exchanged a glance.

"Is this a trick?" Storm said.

"No trick. Well, it is a spell. Get ready." I tossed the skull in the air, unleashed a binding spell that grabbed Storm and Odessa, and wrapped them in a huge hug, just as the skull fell between us, trapping it between our chests.

"What are you doing?" Storm struggled in my grip. Her icy magic sparked between us, but I kept the binding spell tight, so she couldn't move.

"You always say we're stronger together. Our friendship can best anything, including this dark magic." I dug my fingers into their arms, not letting them free.

"You'll be so sorry when I get free. I'll set all my scarecrows on you." Odessa twisted and bucked against my magic.

"You'd better explain yourself," Storm growled. "I don't mind getting a little frost burn by using my magic when we're so close."

"I'll tell you what we're doing. We're destroying this skull and all the darkness in it. We're setting you, the villagers, and the corpses free."

Chapter 18

Storm simply glared at me, while Odessa made protest noises as I tightened the binding spell. A quick look around showed the villagers were closing in, but no one was throwing out the first spell. Maybe they wouldn't cast any magic for fear of hurting Storm and Odessa. But soon enough, someone would take the risk.

"The only dark thing in this place is you," Storm said.

"Focus on the skull. That's the problem, not me. That's what's making you want to kill me."

"This skull is the source of your power?" Storm said.

"Not my power. Storm, sense the magic. That isn't my magic. You know what my power feels like."

"I don't feel so good," Odessa said. "I think Indigo is killing me."

"No! It's not me. And you won't die." At least, I hoped no one was about to die, although the odds weren't in my favor.

"Let us go," Storm yelled in my face.

Her magic fired between us, and I gasped as an icy pain rammed into my stomach. But I wasn't giving up on them. Even as my fingers numbed and my breath plumed out of me in chilled blasts, I had to keep fighting to get through to my closest friends.

My body shuddered as Storm's magic kept hitting me. "Storm, stop! It's the skull. That's the problem."

Odessa jerked in my grip and then groaned, her head dropping down so her chin hit her chest.

"Odessa, fight this magic. I unleashed something from the skull and it's affecting everyone. You're stronger than that and you can fight it," I said. "Think about all the amazing things in your life. Your farm. Your scarecrows. Your amazing pumpkin treats. And your friends. Think about us."

"Stop messing with her," Storm snapped. "We know the truth about you now."

"No, you don't. But I have a feeling you soon will. And if you don't figure this out, then I'm dead. Sense my magic. It isn't coming from the skull." I tightened the binding spell until our faces were squashed together and the skull dug into my chest.

Odessa tried to raise her head, but she was squeezed so tightly against me, she could barely move. "Indigo! What... what are you doing?"

"I've no clue." I said, my mouth jammed right by her ear.

"Why are we all squished up like this?"

My heart pattered out a little hopeful beat. That sounded more like the old Odessa. "Are you back? How do you feel about me?"

"Um... I know we're real good friends, but even this is a bit intimate for my liking."

A relieved laugh blasted out of me. "I'm so happy to hear you say that."

Storm was the next to go. She juddered around, her head jerking back and forth and repeatedly smashing into me.

"Where are we?" Odessa whispered. "I can't see much, but I have a feeling we're not alone. And what the heck is squashed in between us?"

"We're in the cemetery, the entire village is here, the living and the dead, and it's a cursed skull nestled between our bosoms."

Storm stopped head-butting me and slumped forward. She'd have fallen if my binding spell hadn't kept her upright.

Odessa moved her head a fraction. "Did... did I just try to kill you? I feel like I really wanted to kill you a few seconds ago."

"You did. And you probably would have done if I hadn't stopped you," I said. "Everyone here wants to kill me."

"Oh! I don't want to hurt you now. But I got so angry. I was at the farm and got this waft of something rotten. Then I was running as fast as I could. I knew where you were and had to stop you."

"That would be the skull magic making you think like that. And I need your help to destroy it. I've tried everything, but nothing works. My magic isn't strong enough to blast it apart."

"We need Storm's help." Odessa shifted her head. "She's always handy to have around when it comes to destroying things."

"She must have passed out."

"I'll sort that." Odessa licked the side of Storm's face. "Hey! We've got no time to nap. Everyone wants to kill Indigo. Again."

Storm groaned and wriggled. "Get that disgusting tongue away from me."

"Hey, Storm. I just need to check something before I drop this binding spell. Do you want to kill me?"

"No more than usual. What's going on?"

"We have two not so amazing options in front of us. We're about to be attacked by the village mob, or eaten by angry corpses."

Storm's eyes were unfocused as she lifted her head. "More corpses?"

"Yes! And Indigo has a skull wedged between our busts. We have to destroy it," Odessa said.

Storm frowned. "How will we do that? Crush it with our mighty cleavages?"

"I'll explain everything later. Do you both trust me?" I said.

They nodded as best they could.

"Then let's do this. You need to open your magic to me. We have to do this together."

"We're always better together," Odessa said. "Take everything you need from me."

"One question before we do this. Did I just try to freeze you to death?" Storm said.

"Yep, and I have the numb toes to prove it," I said.

"Same here," Odessa said. "I won't be happy if I get chilblains."

"You're lucky your head is still on your shoulders," Storm said. "Uh... sorry about that."

"Don't worry about it. Think about the skull. Once it's gone, I'm hoping the corpses will go back in their coffins and the villagers won't want to destroy me."

"I feel like I've missed a few things," Storm said.

"I promise, I'll tell you everything. Are you both ready?"

They nodded again.

I loosened the binding spell a fraction so our hands and arms were free. We linked hands and formed a circle. The skull dropped to the ground and rested between our feet.

"How about using a destruction spell?" Odessa said.

"We're too close. It could rebound onto us." I glanced at the glaring villagers and groaning corpses. "We need fire, ice, and strength. I can conjure a stream of fire."

"I've got the ice," Storm said.

Odessa reached into her pocket and pulled out a black velvet pouch. "And I've got my powdered pumpkin to make everything go with a sucker-punch bang."

I blocked out the distractions, hoped no one would jump me from behind, and we evoked our individual streams of magic.

My fire heated the air, but I kept tight control over the jet of flames so we wouldn't get singed. Storm snaked a ring of ice around the jet and hovered it over the skull, while Odessa held a full hand of glowing pumpkin powder over our magic streams.

She dropped the powder just as the ice and fire met. Power blasted out of us and smashed into the skull.

It wobbled from side to side and let out an ear-splitting shriek.

I gritted my teeth, my ears ringing from the sound, but kept on going. The skull glowed red and vibrated.

"Give it more magic!" I yelled. "It's working."

A quick glance at Storm and Odessa showed they weren't holding back. Odessa was shaking and panting, and Storm had her teeth bared as sweat trickled down her face.

"It's about to blow," Storm said. "Look out!"

I let out a final blast of my magic and turned my head as the skull shattered into tiny bone fragments. I pulled back my power and looked around the cemetery. The corpses were dropping to the ground, and all the villagers stood still, looking shocked, as if they weren't sure how they found themselves to be in the cemetery.

"We did it!" Odessa grabbed me in a tight hug.

I dropped the binding magic around us and hugged her back. "Thanks to your help." I grabbed Storm and included her in the hug, even though she grumbled.

"I'm still not sure what happened," Storm said. "Why is everyone here? And what's with this skull?"

"I'll tell you everything back at the house. I've had more than enough of this cemetery."

Russell swooped down and landed on my shoulder. He tapped the top of my head several times.

"Are we friends again?" I reached up to stroke him. "And do you remember what an amazing familiar you are?"

He cawed, nuzzled my face, and flew around my head.

"What trouble have you been getting into this time?" Nugget trotted over with Hilda riding on his back.

I scooped them up and gave them a hug. "Am I glad to see you two. And you're both yourselves."

"Who else would we be?" Nugget said. "Although I do have a question. Why is Olympus sleeping on our couch?"

I grinned. "That's another story. Come on, let's get out of here."

"Um... before we do that, you should take a look at what's left of the skull." Odessa stood by the remains of the skull, tugging on her bottom lip.

I turned to see a red mist rising out of the fragments, and my happy mood instantly died. I settled Nugget and Hilda back on the ground and watched as the red mist swirled up into a spiral.

"That's not good," Storm said. "The skull's magic should have been destroyed when we blasted it into pieces."

"Did we get it wrong? We didn't destroy it, but we let something out?" Odessa said.

"I've seen this mist before," I said. "It's been following me around Witch Haven. And it's time to find out what it wants."

"What shall we do about the villagers?" Odessa said.

Several people were wandering away, looking bemused, but most of them just stood around scratching their heads or mumbling to their neighbor.

"Let's keep them out of the way, in case this turns nasty. Check they have their memories back and don't want to kill me, though. We don't want any surprise attacks while we're dealing with whatever this is." I gestured at the red mist.

"I'll do crowd control," Odessa said.

I nodded, my attention on the mist as it swirled around. It was forming a vaguely human shape.

"We should just blast it again," Storm said. "If it forms a solid shape, it could cause more trouble."

"I want to know what this is. I'm certain this mist is connected to the coven that ruined Magda's life and messed with me when I was a teenager. I have to know who's behind it."

Storm nodded and flexed her fingers. "You just say the word, and I'm happy to blast away. I've still got some magic left."

My smile was grateful as I patted her arm. Storm was back to her old self, and I could always count on her to thump anything that needed thumping.

Odessa hurried back to join us. "Everyone is fine, although they're all confused. But they have no murderous intentions toward you. I put out the word that a toxic fog from the river floated across the village and has been making people hallucinate."

"Smart idea. I had no clue how to explain all of this," I said.

"Most of them aren't moving, though. And they want to know what we're doing."

"That's a great question," I said. "We're... investigating."

"More like, we're about to get ourselves killed," Storm said.

I bit my lip. "We might. If you want to leave—"

"Oh, hush up. What's a little mortal danger among friends?" Storm smirked at me.

"That mist looks human," Odessa said. "Is something trying to come through?"

I kept watching the mist. It was definitely forming the shape of a slender female, wearing a long, floor-length dress.

"So, we meet again," a voice said from the mist as the figure continued to form.

I recognized that voice. It was the ghost from Luna's apartment. "I thought I'd gotten rid of you."

"No, you didn't. You knew I was still around. And you knew I wouldn't go without seeing you first."

"Why does she want to see you?" Odessa whispered.

I shrugged. "No idea. Did you take Luna?"

"I did. I find her fascinating. I've been keeping her in a little place called limbo."

Odessa jabbed a finger in my side. "I knew it. I said that's where we'd find her."

I nodded, my focus still on the shape.

"I watched you while you attempted to find her," the misty figure said. "You have power. You haven't let down the Ash witch legacy."

"Give her back to us," I said. "She's of no use to you."

"I wouldn't say that. And Luna called to me. I was certain I could convince her to join my coven."

"What do you mean, she called to you?" Storm said.

The mist continued to form a female shape, although the facial features were still indistinct.

"Your friend's particular thirst attracted my attention."

"Thirst? You mean, the amount of herbal tea she drinks?" I said.

The mysterious woman laughed. "I couldn't convince her to come over to my side. Luna's strong. She makes a good friend for you. I'm pleased you found her."

"Why do you care who my friends are?" I had that same faint niggle in the back of my head that I knew this magic user.

"I'm done with this getting to know you rubbish," Storm said. "We've destroyed your skull, we've ruined your plans, now give us our friend back."

"I intend to keep her," the woman said. "Unless you give me something I need."

"What's that?" I said.

"My lost love."

Storm snorted a laugh. "You want us to find you a date?"

Flickers of jagged, dark energy shot through the mist. "You're carrying the only thing that will bring me back my paramour. You took him from me, and I insist you bring him back."

"You mean the ghost jar?" I said. "Did we trap your boyfriend in Luna's apartment?"

A soft breeze swirled around us. It carried that same tang of rot I'd smelt in the cemetery when fighting the corpses.

"Killion let himself down. I thought he was stronger than that, but you somehow managed to capture him."

"You really want to date a guy who can't take care of himself?" Storm said.

The dark flickers in the mist grew hectic. "We weren't expecting such resistance. We didn't anticipate you could control your powers. You've had so little education."

"She's talking like she knows you," Odessa said.

Uneasiness curled around my spine. "We don't know each other."

"I know you, Indigo. Which is why you're still alive. And I'm prepared to offer you a trade."

"A trade?" I tilted my head.

"I'll return Luna if you summon Killion to me."

No one spoke for several seconds.

"Is that a good idea?" Odessa whispered.

"We have to get Luna back," Storm said.

"But the ghosts in Luna's apartment weren't fun to tangle with. If these two get back together, they'll cause chaos."

I narrowed my eyes at the mysterious woman. I still couldn't make out her face. "We don't have Killion. The ghost jar was destroyed. He's escaped."

"I know that. I took the ghost jar and tried to extract him, but something went wrong. His energy was weak from being trapped, and he slipped through my fingers."

"That was careless," I said. "You can't have thought much of him if you dropped him."

Storm smirked. "Maybe don't rile the evil mist too much. I doubt she plays nice."

I shrugged. "If Killion is so weak, how do you expect us to get him back? He could be anywhere."

"You must return him to me. I am lost without him." A hint of desperation colored the woman's voice. "And if you fail, you'll never see Luna again."

I turned to Storm and Odessa. "We have to do this."

"We can't trust that man-obsessed thing," Storm said. "What if we give her that creepy ghost lover and she vanishes?"

"I won't disappear," she said. "I have no wish to double-cross those I care about."

My stomach flipped, and I turned back to the misty woman. "We'll summon him back in exchange for Luna, but you need to answer a question before we do anything to help you."

She spread out her arms. "Ask me anything. Much like Magda's journals, my life is an open book."

That was it. It confirmed she knew a lot more about me than I did her. "How do you know me?"

Her face shimmered into view.

My heart dropped to my boots, my throat tightened, and my vision blurred.

Odessa squeaked. "Indigo, she looks just like you."

I stared at the floating image before me, my lungs burning because I'd forgotten how to breathe. "That's because she's my mom."

Chapter 19

I'd have hit the ground if Odessa and Storm weren't holding onto me. I stared at the image again, my heart thudding so fast I grew dizzy. This had to be a trick. My mom couldn't be behind the darkness in Witch Haven.

"That's not the welcome I'd hoped for. Aren't you going to come kiss your mother?" The fully formed, misty woman smiled, but it held no kindness.

I shook my head. "You're... you're not her. She's dead. She died giving birth to me."

"Not true. I was close to death when I gave birth to you, but I lived for a short time afterward."

I tried to get my thoughts in order, but they refused to obey. I had a hundred questions tumbling through my head and no clue where to start.

"Is that really your mom?" Odessa whispered.

"No, this is the dark magic messing with us," I croaked out.

"Again, false. I loved you and your father greatly. I couldn't bear the thought of letting you go, and I wasn't ready to give up on the life we'd made. We were so looking forward to welcoming our first child into the world." There was a glimmer of sadness in her eyes.

"She looks just like the pictures I've seen of her," Odessa said.

I nodded, too stunned to form a sentence.

My mom sighed. "There were complications during the labor, and I lost a lot of blood. Your father and I performed healing magic, but I kept on getting weaker. Nothing we did could reverse the damage. And as you know, magic should never interfere with the natural order of life and death."

I shook my head. "You died. We had a funeral for you." I didn't remember it, but as I'd grown up, I sometimes visited my mom's grave. She'd died to give me life, so I'd always felt a connection to her.

"You did. And I witnessed all of that. And for a short time, I was dead. But then I saw the light. Or rather, I was introduced to the wonderful darkness. Killion came to me when I was laid out in the mortuary."

"And what, he offered to bring you back as some kind of twisted spirit in exchange for joining him?" I said.

"I'm alive, not a ghost. I'm just not fully in this world." She smiled. "He's a wonderful man. He taught me the true power of magic. And it doesn't lie on the path you follow."

Anger pulsed through me. "He's not a man. No man would bring back a dead woman."

"He could be a demon," Odessa said.

"Or an ancient ghost," Storm said. "They get powerful when they've been around a few thousand years."

"Whatever he is, he seduced you with darkness." I scowled at my mom. "How could you go from loving Dad to a monster?"

She arched an eyebrow. "You're lecturing me on bad choices when it comes to men?"

"I have to. Most people don't get their heads turned by evil."

My mom laughed. "It seems we're both drawn to inappropriate men."

"I... you mean Olympus? I'm not drawn to him."

"A mother knows. And I see the attachment growing between you. You can't help who you fall in love with. I love Killion passionately, and I'll do anything to get him back."

"You've failed so far," Storm said.

"Which is why I need my daughter's help. Indigo captured him. She can bring him back. She has the pieces of the ghost jar that connect to him. Her magic will reunite us."

"And create a crazy duo who'll go on a killing spree," I said.

"No, I'll leave the killing sprees to the woman who stole my husband and my wonderful daughter." My mom's eyes glowed with an unnatural intensity. "You did such an incredible job. I only wish you'd fulfilled the prophecy and emptied the entire village of its inhabitants. Then the way would have been clear for me and Killion to take our place in Witch Haven. We could have ruled together with darkness. We'd have been a complete family."

I couldn't get air into my lungs as it took me a second to process everything she'd just told me. "It was you! You and Killion were behind the dark magic that infected me and Magda. You set us loose to destroy this whole place?"

"You were perfectly positioned to carry out my wishes. You had yet to come into your full power, so were easy to manipulate. And Magda deserved no less. I wasn't even cold on the mortuary slab before she was knocking on the door and offering sympathetic hugs. She couldn't wait to get her feet under the table and take on the role of wife and perfect mother to you."

"Magda didn't do that."

"Your father married her before I'd been dead a year."

"Because he loved her. And Magda was an amazing mom to me. I couldn't have wished for any better," I said. "You destroyed everything I had because you were jealous?"

"You were my family. I wanted to keep you. Magda didn't deserve you."

"You're not so perfect," Storm said. "Killion turned your head quickly enough, and you were happy to run off with your demon lover boy as soon as he clicked his wicked fingers. If you loved your real family, you'd never have been swayed by darkness."

She glowered at Storm. "Watch your tongue, Winter witch. I know things about you. Things that'll change how your friends see you. You're not so pure."

"Nothing you tell us about Storm will stop us from loving her," Odessa said.

My mom's gaze flicked to Odessa. "Ah, and the pumpkin princess. You're not so innocent, either."

Odessa's cheeks flushed. "I also have nothing to hide."

Storm's face paled, but she stood firm. "And I have no secrets."

My mom chuckled. "You both hide plenty. You should be careful what you conceal. As you've seen with Luna, hiding too much from others attracts the wrong kind of interest."

I still had no clue what she was talking about. Luna's magic was all about food. There was nothing dark about that.

I glanced at Storm and Odessa and saw them share a look. It seemed they didn't share that belief.

"What will it be, Indigo?" My mom tilted her head. "Your best friend for my one true love?"

I'd never known my birth mom, but I'd heard plenty about her and I'd seen tons of pictures, so I felt like I knew her. And she was my blood. She was another Ash witch. There were so many conflicting emotions whirling inside me, I didn't know which one to settle on.

But I had to focus on what was important. Luna was my family, too. This misty, broken form of a witch may have been my birth mom, but that was our only link. She wasn't my real family, she'd never cared for me, and she'd been broken by dark magic and then used it against the family she should have protected.

"We agree to your deal," I said. "If you return Luna, we'll do everything we can to bring Killion back so you can be reunited with him."

I looked at Storm and Odessa again, and they both nodded, although their expressions were grim.

"Agreed. And I'll be glad to relieve myself of your friend. Luna's powers aren't to be messed with."

"I hope she's given you hell," I said. "It's no less than you deserve. And one more thing."

My mom lifted her eyebrows, an amused expression on her face. "What's that?"

"Leave Witch Haven alone. You've done enough damage. This place needs to be left in peace."

"But it's ripe for the taking. Everyone here is so bitter and jaded. Their negativity is the perfect environment for us to thrive."

"It's only like that because you've been messing with the village. Leave, and everyone will be happy again," I said. "And Magda and my dad raised me well. As an Ash witch, I know justice always prevails. You may keep trying to get Witch Haven, but you will fail, because you're in the wrong."

A flicker of rage crossed my mom's face, but then she laughed again. "You have my spirit. Perhaps there is a place for you at my side."

"I'll never join you. I have all the family I need right here. There's no place for you in my life, and there's no room for you and Killion in Witch Haven."

Her smile faded, and she flicked a hand at me. "Get on with it. Return Killion to me, before I start picking off the nosy villagers."

I extracted the pieces of ghost jar from my bag and held them out in my palm. "Are you both ready for this?" I said to Storm and Odessa.

"Ready to bring back some insane ghost demon creature who'll most likely terrorize us?" Storm grinned. "Bring it on." She placed a hand over mine.

"We've come this far," Odessa said. "What's one more unstable dark magic user in the village? No offense, Indigo."

"None taken. And I'm nothing like my mom. I won't be swayed by her darkness. Let's get lover boy back and bring Luna home."

Chapter 20

"I feel his approach," my mom said. "Keep channeling your energy into the jar fragments. Summon my love back to me."

"She needs to put a sock in it," Storm growled.

We'd been summoning Killion for almost an hour. All three of us were sweating and shaking with the effort. His energy was out there, but it was diffuse and weak, and he didn't seem able to reconnect all the pieces to materialize.

"We have to take a break," Odessa whispered. "I'm about to pass out."

"Keep going a bit longer. This is for Luna. We have to get this ghost demon back, so we can save her. No Killion, no Luna."

"And then that's it, and this is over?" Storm said. "You think those two will flit off happily and never cause us any more problems?"

"No, not from the way my mom is talking," I said. "But one problem at a time. Let's get Luna back. We'll be stronger when we have her here."

"You're losing focus," my mom snapped. "If you don't pay attention, my love will drift away. And if you don't return him to me, you'll never see Luna again."

"We get it." Storm rolled her shoulders and steadied her shaking hands.

We all focused on the pieces of ghost jar I held.

Hilda climbed up my leg and settled on my shoulder. "You can't keep on using your magic without resting. You'll get sick if you empty your reserves. A witch can only keep casting magic for so long before it becomes dangerous for her. I sense that you're fading."

"You heard my crazy mom," I said. "This is for Luna."

"Yes, but you'll die if you don't stop. Luna wouldn't want you to sacrifice yourself for her."

"I should. My birth mom is behind all this." I glanced at her. She was swirling around, her impatience clear as she waited for her twisted lover to return. "I really thought she was dead."

"We all did," Hilda said. "But you're nothing like her. You're so much better than her. And she's not even a real witch anymore. I've been trying to get a read on her energy and keep getting a muddle of different powers. She's trapped between this world and the next, and there is so much dark magic pulsing out of her that I feel sick. She's damaging to be around."

"Perhaps that's why she wants to get her hands on Witch Haven," I said. "She needs an anchor. A place to ground the darkness."

"And cause even more destruction," Storm said. "We're not letting that happen."

"We have to get rid of her," I muttered. "But she won't go until Killion is here."

"We've got nothing more to give you," Hilda said. "I wish I could offer you more of my energy, but I'm running on empty."

"No, you've all done more than enough." Nugget and Russell were panting and slumped on the ground beside my feet. Having familiars meant I got an extra power boost, but it was at their expense. The more I kept blasting summoning magic into the ghost jar fragments, the weaker everyone became.

"Bring me back my love," my mom yelled.

I gritted my teeth and gave it one final push. Sweat dripped down the side of my face as I channelled my magic into bringing back this twisted energy.

A roar of pure rage filled the air. I staggered back as my magic died and the connection with Storm and Odessa was lost.

"He's here." My mom raced toward a misty image a few feet away.

I slumped to the ground on my knees and dropped the pieces of ghost jar. Storm and Odessa joined me. We could do nothing but kneel, pant, and try not to faint.

"We did it. We summoned back the bad guy," Storm said.

I looked up to see my mom embracing a jagged ball of energy. She was whispering and stroking it. And slowly, the image of a tall blond man appeared. He was kind of Viking handsome. Tall with muscles, and an arrogant sneer on his face as his gaze flicked over to us.

He floated toward me, my mom's hand clasped in his. "You're the witch who captured me?"

I staggered to my feet and did a mock curtsy. "I'm happy to be of service. I'm just sorry I didn't destroy you."

"She doesn't mean that, my love," my mom said hastily. "This is my daughter, Indigo."

Killion said nothing, but his sneer said everything.

My gaze moved to my mom. "Where is Luna? We had a deal."

"You made a deal? Without consulting me?" Killion's sharp gaze settled on my mom.

"To get you back. And it was worth the sacrifice. I've been testing new recruits for our coven, but the witch I chose wasn't suitable. She was difficult and stubborn, and kept saying she wanted to come back to her friends and family."

I grinned. "That's Luna for you. She's awesome. And she'd never be swayed by what you had to offer."

"You shouldn't be so quick to judge," my mom said. "Luna was tempted. She's been tempted for a long time. Still, we all have our secrets. Each and every one of us." Her gaze swept over the exhausted group.

"Enough of the secrets talk," I said. "Give us back our friend."

"You shouldn't bend to this witch's demands," Killion said.

"Forget the witches, my darling. We have a lot of catching up to do." My mom placed a kiss on Killion's lips.

I grimaced and looked away.

She clicked her fingers as she continued to kiss Killion. A cold, gray mist swirled around her, and a few seconds later, Luna appeared. She fell to her knees and hunched over, gasping.

We raced over and surrounded her in a protective circle. Odessa helped her to her feet, while I kept an eye on my mom and her creepy lover, who were still locked in an embarrassingly intense embrace.

"Is Luna okay?" I said, my back to her as I guarded her against my mom and Killion.

"She seems to be," Odessa said. "Luna, do you know where you are? Do you know who I am?"

"I... I think so. I've been trying so hard to get back here." Luna's voice was shaky, but it was definitely her.

"Get Luna away from here," I said. "I have unfinished business with a family member."

"Are you sure that's a good idea?" Odessa whispered. "While she's distracted, we should get out of here."

I nodded, my glare fixed on my mom, who was finally done making out with Killion. I glanced over my shoulder, relieved to see they were moving back.

Luna looked like she'd lost weight and her hair was bedraggled, but she gave me a weak smile.

"It's time for us to leave," my mom said.

I turned back to her. "Good. You're done here."

She huffed out a laugh. "Whatever makes you think that?"

"Witch Haven doesn't want you. You've been trying to get your claws into it for over a decade, and you've failed."

Her gaze flitted around the cemetery. "I've far from failed. From what I hear, the Magic Council is thinking of destroying this place because it has become so tainted with my darkness."

"Our darkness," Killion said.

"Of course. Our darkness." Mom kissed his cheek.

I grimaced. I hated a domineering guy. "The Magic Council won't need to destroy the village if you leave it alone."

"It's my home. I deserve this after everything that happened to me."

"I'm sorry giving birth to me cost you your life. I wanted the same things as you, to have a mom and a dad who loved me. I wanted you in my life, but it didn't work out that way. Tragedies happen all the time. You have to accept that and move on."

"I didn't deserve that. I should have been saved. Your father's magic failed me. He didn't want me to live. He wanted Magda. He as good as killed me."

"Mom! He loved you. And magic can't solve everything. Sometimes, bad things just happen," I said. "And... although Dad cared for Magda, he never forgot you. I sometimes think he died of a broken heart because he never got over losing you. He tried hard to make a happy life for me, that's why he married so soon after your death, but I could see how broken he was. He was broken because you died. He never stopped loving you."

A dozen different expressions crossed my mom's face. She clung to Killion's arm as if she might fall if she let him go.

"Is your child always so wilful?" Killion said. "Perhaps we don't want her to join us if she's always going to talk back. I insist on obedience in my coven."

I choked out a laugh, not sure I'd heard him right. "Join you? I won't ever join you."

My mom held out her hand. "Of course you will. I've been hoping you'd come to your senses and realize where your destiny lies, but all this time you've fought me. You keep trying to save this tired little place. It's time for change. The darkness needs to take control."

"You're wrong. Witch Haven is an amazing place, and it doesn't need you spoiling it. Leave it alone."

Her eyes narrowed. "Then come with us. We can have adventures together. You're my daughter. You should be with me."

"No, I shouldn't. My family is right here." I looked at my friends and familiars, who were huddled together watching my every move. "I have a great life here, and you're not ruining it. You got what you wanted. You destroyed Magda, and you nearly destroyed me, all because you couldn't bear to see the man you cared about happy with another woman."

Killion growled under his breath.

"You're the man I love now," my mom said to him. She looked back at me, a hint of desperation in her eyes. "You'll soon see how much more powerful you can be when you embrace your dark side. You had a taste when you were seventeen and you touched the dark magic I put in Magda's care. It gave you so much."

"It gave me nothing! It corrupted me, and I hurt people I cared about. This village hates me because of the damage I caused. They'll never forgive me, and I don't blame them. And I deserved the punishment I got. But I've changed, and I'll never touch dark magic again. I don't want to be with you."

"We can recruit new members to the coven from other places," Killion muttered. "And we don't need your daughter. If she won't come willingly, she'll only slow us down."

"Don't bother gathering new recruits," I said. "You failed to recruit Luna, and you'll keep on failing. Magic users don't want your power."

"Then they're fools," Killion said. "We offer unlimited power. Everything you could desire."

"I have everything I desire right here. You can offer me nothing else."

My mom shot out a hand, and her fingers curled. "You will come with us. If I have to drag you away from this sorry little place on your knees, then that's what I'll do."

It like a vice had wrapped around my neck. I wheezed out a breath as my mom's sharp magic wove around me.

"No! You can't have her," Odessa yelled. "She's our friend. Let her go!"

Three separate blasts of magic shot out either side of me as my friends' power slammed into my mom and Killion.

Killion shot back an arc of silver magic as my mom continued to drag me toward her.

I added my own magic to the mix, despite my throat burning and the desire to do nothing more than find a way to breathe. But my power was weak, and I had barely anything left to fight with.

There was a blur of movement above me, and Russell shot out of the air and landed on Killion's head, squawking and pecking at him. A second later, Nugget joined in and leaped on my mom in a hissing ball of fluffed up fury.

I redirected my magic, pulsing it into my familiars so they could grow huge and even more fearsome.

My mom shrieked, and her hold on me wavered, but she blasted Nugget away with a spell, then focused her evil intentions back on me. "You will come with us. I'm not leaving without you. I've invested too much of my time to give up on you now. I changed Witch Haven for you. You need a dark paradise to dwell in and thrive. This has always been about you."

"This has nothing to do with me. This is about fulfilling your own twisted desires. And I'd rather die than be with you," I said.

"That can be arranged." Killion batted at Russell. "Destroy her. There are other places we can infiltrate. Places that are less trouble."

"This is my home," my mom growled out. "This is the place I should control with my daughter by my side."

"This place is more trouble than it's worth," Killion said.

"You should listen to him," I said. "He's talking sense. Leave Witch Haven. We don't want you."

"I don't care what you want. I'm taking you." Mom's magic rammed into me, punching a blast of rank smelling energy into my chest. I yelped as fire and ice rushed through me and black dots flooded my vision.

A chant began among the watching villagers, and my eyes widened as I recognized their words. They were all speaking the banishing spell.

My gaze shot around the cemetery. Everyone had joined hands, and they were chanting. The living and the dead were all involved, with the corpses back on their feet. They were helping me.

They finished the words of the spell, and a pulse of magic shot across the cemetery and blasted into my mom and Killion.

They jerked like they'd been hit by a bolt of electricity and were then lifted into the air.

Half a dozen corpses walked over, grabbed their arms and legs, and dragged them out of the cemetery.

The villagers kept repeating the banishing spell and pulsing magic into them. I joined in, adding my own fading power, still shocked to the core to get their help. Tears sprung into my eyes, but they were happy tears. All this time, I'd been hiding from the villagers, certain they hated me for what I'd done to them, but they'd just saved my life and prevented my mom from dragging me into her dark coven.

I was almost knocked to the ground when three pairs of arms wrapped around me, and I staggered under the weight of my friends' fierce embrace.

I turned and hugged Luna first. "How are you doing?"

"I'm exhausted. But so glad to be back." Dark circles sat under her eyes, but the wide smile on her face made her beautiful.

Odessa grinned. "We got rid of the darkness."

I looked at the cemetery gates, where I could just make out my mom as she was pulled away by the corpses. "They'll never be able to come back again. Everyone's magic has banished them. The second they try to enter Witch Haven, they'll be rejected."

Storm nodded. "No one wants them here. And the villagers all heard the truth about you. They know you and Magda weren't to blame for what happened."

"You had no control over that," Luna said. "Your mom and Killion are terrible people for what they've done to you."

I hugged her again, happy tears dampening my cheeks. "Did they hurt you?"

"They weren't kind to me, but I'll survive."

"Luna!" Albert rushed through the crowd, his expression one of shock and disbelief. "Is it really you?"

"Uncle!" She threw herself into his arms and they both laughed and cried and talked over each other.

Odessa slung an arm around my shoulders, while Storm gave me a fist bump.

Russell, Hilda, and Nugget joined us, and I gave them all a well-done-for-being-awesome-familiars pet.

I looked around the cemetery and saw several people nod and smile at me as they slowly left through the gates.

It was so overwhelming, and I couldn't stop from happy crying and smiling. I was finally accepted here again. I had a place to call home, and I'd never felt so content.

"What shall we do now?" Odessa said.

Luna pulled back from hugging Albert. "I don't know about all of you, but I need a cake and a sit down. Limbo was no fun. And they don't serve desserts."

"I can arrange that. You can eat dessert day and night." Albert hugged her tight.

I smiled as we all linked arms and left the cemetery, feeling safe and happy in my friends' warm embrace.

Chapter 21

I sat back in my seat in the bakery, content to listen to my friends talk and laugh with each other. Nugget was snoring under the table, and Russell and Hilda were snuggled on a chair, snoozing after indulging in treats and exhausted from so much intense magic use.

We'd been here all day since leaving the chaotic events of the cemetery, and it was already dark outside. I was shattered, but so happy to have Luna back.

Best of all, all the villagers were back to normal, and Luna's uncle was his usual warm, sweet self, and kept checking to make sure we didn't want for anything.

"You've got incoming," Storm muttered. "You'd better get used to being popular around here."

I looked up to see Cornelia Norwood approaching with a gift in her hands. This had been happening all day. People kept coming over to apologize for their behavior and give me presents.

Cornelia stopped and adjusted her eye patch. She held out the gift. "I just wanted to thank you for what you've done for us. It's been such a long time since I felt normal that it feels weird. Everyone saw what you did in the cemetery, and we're so grateful. Witch Haven finally feels safe again."

I accepted the gift. It was a small velvet pouch, and inside was a piece of amethyst. "Thanks. This is beautiful, but you don't need to give me anything. I was just trying to make up for what I did. Set things right."

"I saw you wearing something similar, so I thought you liked that stone."

I touched my bare neck. Magda's necklace had given me the strength to believe in myself. But in truth, I hadn't needed it. I trusted my magic now.

"I'll make this into something stunning," I said.

"I'd gotten used to feeling angry and bitter and wanting to cause harm. That's been lifted because of you. If ever you need anything from my inn, you come and ask. And you'll never have to pay for a thing."

"I'm just glad I could help get Witch Haven back to normal." I wasn't comfortable about everyone thanking me and giving me things. After all, it was my birth mom who'd done this, and I'd been her vessel. Along with Magda, we'd made a mess of things. But I'd put it right, and although it would take a while for it to feel normal to walk through the village and not get yelled at for being an evil witch, it was something I was looking forward to.

Cornelia said goodbye and hurried away.

"You'll have to get used to being a celebrity," Storm said.

"People will forget about what happened soon," I said.

"Not likely," Luna said. "I was talking to my uncle, and they're thinking about making a statue of you and putting it in the middle of the village."

I groaned. "Please say that's a joke."

Odessa chuckled. "It's a great idea. The magnificent Indigo Ash. She saved Witch Haven from the darkness and brought her best friend back so she could eat cake once again."

Luna wiped cake crumbs off her shirt. "It was so worth it. This cake has never tasted so good. Absence definitely makes the cake taste amazing."

I studied Luna for a few seconds. "My mom spoke about why she tried to recruit you to her coven."

Luna's gaze dropped to her plate. "What did she say?"

"She mentioned your particular thirst and said it drew her to you. What was she talking about?"

Luna glanced around the group, then stuffed a piece of iced bun in her mouth and chewed. "No idea. We need more cake. I'll go get it." She hopped up and hurried to the counter.

"Do either of you think that was weird?" I said.

Odessa nodded as she sprinkled powdered pumpkin over her cake. "Maybe Luna needs time to readjust. Being in limbo must mess with your head."

Storm shrugged. "I'm just glad she's back. I don't care if she is a bit weird."

I leaned back in my seat again and nursed my mug of coffee. Maybe there was nothing to it, but I wanted to know why my mom was so interested in recruiting Luna to the darkness. And I hadn't forgotten Magda's words. You can't always trust the ones you love. Maybe that had been a warning about my mom, but maybe it also had something to do with my best friend.

Silvaria marched into the bakery. She had Shamrock over her shoulder as she strode to the table.

I stood and narrowed my eyes at her. "Surprised to see me alive after you ran out on me again?"

"Always. I don't know how you manage it." She dumped Shamrock on the floor and looked at Odessa. "I believe this is yours. I found him in my cemetery."

Odessa knelt and stroked Shamrock's face. "My beautiful boy. What happened to you?"

"He saved me from the corpses," I said. "I owe Shamrock. Do you think you can put him back together?"

Odessa didn't look up as she nodded. "My boy will be good as new once I get him back to the farm."

"I should have burned him. Big old waste of space." Silvaria turned to go.

I caught hold of her arm. "You'd never do that. You have a heart hiding in that chest."

She tugged my arm out of her grip. "That's none of your business."

"I'm making it my business. And we need to find a dance class."

Her eyes widened. "A... dance class? Are you serious?"

"Yep. Even though you didn't stick to your end of the bargain, we both need some fun after what we've been through. What will it be: ballet, hip-hop, or salsa?"

Her stern expression softened. "Belly dance. I've always wanted to be a belly dancer."

"Then let's do that. I'll find the class, you get the floaty veils, and we'll get shaking our bits."

Silvaria pursed her lips. "I'll let you know when I'm free." She left the bakery, shaking her head.

"Dancing? With Silvaria?" Odessa stared up at me.

I nodded as I sat down. "She needs something to look forward to. Being around the dead all the time can't be good for a person."

"Look out! Jerk alert," Storm said.

I looked over my shoulder and sat up straight. Olympus was striding toward the table.

"Limpy's not a jerk." Odessa thumped Storm's leg. "Indigo, do you want us to leave you alone?"

"No, you stay here. I'll go see him."

"Be good," Odessa said.

"Just remember, play it cool. Guys hate it when you're too keen," Storm said.

I walked over to Olympus, my heart beating a little too fast for my liking. "So, have you decided on a date for our wedding?"

His cheeks flushed, and he cleared his throat several times. "About that. We need to talk."

I gasped. "Don't say you're breaking up with me? I've put a deposit on a dress. And the eight-tier cake is on order."

"You're not funny," he grumbled. "You do know it was the magic your mom blasted out across the cemetery that did that to me?"

I frowned. "Does that mean you don't want to make me Mrs. Duke?"

Olympus tugged at his collar. "Will you hate me if I say no?"

I laughed. "You're off the hook. We haven't even been on a date. Although you were really into having a big wedding. Are you sure there's not an idea about getting married in the back of your mind?"

He relaxed and laughed along with me. "Maybe one day, but perhaps I should officially ask you out first. If that's something you'd be interested in?"

I'd never seen Olympus look so awkward and out of his depth. It was sort of endearing. "It's probably a good idea to see if we actually like each other, before you put a ring on it. Why not? Let's see what happens."

"Great. And I do remember some of the things you said when I was chasing you around like a love sick puppy. No flowers, no scented candles, and basically no romance."

"Well, not no romance, but ease off on the cheesy romance, and we'll be fine."

He reached for my hand and gave it a squeeze. "I'll get to work on that. And how are you? I've been at the Magic Council for the last hour getting an update. I got here as quickly as I could. I was worried about you."

"I'm... probably in shock. I still can't believe my mom and her creepy boyfriend were behind this."

"You do know who Killion is?"

"A seriously bad guy?"

"The prince of demons."

"My birth mom hooked up with a prince?"

Olympus arched an eyebrow. "You seemed to have not heard the demon part."

"Oh, I did. But why choose my mom to be with him?"

"Because of her magic. Add an Ash witch to his coven and it doubles his power."

"Demons have covens?"

"Demons have... gangs? Groupies? I'm not sure how to describe it." He touched my cheek. "The Magic Council is all over this. They've been hunting Killion for decades. They'll stop him."

"And my mom?"

"Most likely. Are you good with that?"

"Yes! She's nothing to me."

"Are you sure?"

"I... well, I hesitated for a second. She's the only blood family I have left, but how can I love her? She did all this to our home."

"She's gone now. And so is Killion. And if they try to get back in, I'll know about it. You're safe here."

I smiled up at him and then looked back at my friends. "I have no doubts about that."

The bakery door crashed open and Monty bounded in. He was followed by Fire Fang.

Olympus scowled. "I told you to stay in the office."

Monty wagged his tail and licked Olympus' hands. "You didn't mean that. And I found my new friend in the alley. He was chasing a bunch of angry gnomes."

Fire Fang growled and his eyes glowed red.

Storm hollered his name, and he loped over to the table.

Olympus shook his head at Monty. "Be quiet and behave."

"Always. I'm an excellent familiar. Oooh! Is that meringue?" He bounded over the counter and rested his paws on the top.

"I should turn him back into a toy. He's so much easier to control."

"No! Monty is great. He's perfect for you." I rested a hand on Olympus' chest. "And I haven't forgotten about Bloom. I will help you figure out what happened to her."

"Thanks, but I'm still not sure who has her. I've been hearing what your mom said when she was in the cemetery. It doesn't make sense she'd recruit someone so young to her coven. Bloom only has basic magic because of her age."

"We'll figure it out. And we'll do it together."

He leaned forward and kissed my cheek. "Yes. We'll do it together. And I've already begun collecting statements from the villagers about what you did to keep Witch Haven safe. I'll be presenting a case in front of the Magic Council as soon as I can."

"Do you think they'll listen?" Hope fluttered in my chest.

"Of course. We'll come to an arrangement about you keeping the house and the debts you owe. And there won't be any charges brought against you. You've saved Witch Haven. The Magic Council owes you. And I'll make sure you get to call in that favor. Your place is here, with all of us. You deserve no less."

I could have kissed his face right off for saying that. Instead, I did the grown-up thing. "Come and join us. Since we're dating, I need to make sure my friends approve of you."

Olympus glanced at the table. Storm and Odessa were staring at him intently, and Luna was just returning with a tray of cakes. He swallowed loudly. "I'm not sure I'll ever pass their tests."

I dragged him to the table. "You will. Just be prepared to be thoroughly interrogated."

A smile crossed his face as he looked at me. "What have I gotten myself into?"

"The most fun you're ever going to have."

Odessa grabbed another seat and set it down for Olympus. "Hi, Limpy. I'm so excited about being a bridesmaid at your wedding."

"Wedding?" Luna said. "Who's getting married?"

I laughed. "There's so much we still need to catch you up on. How about I get more coffee and I'll tell you all about the terrible marriage proposal Olympus made to me?"

He dropped his head into his hands. "I was under the influence of very strong magic when I made that proposal."

"Yeah, yeah, you can't use that excuse on me," I said.

"You have to stick to your end of the deal." Storm's expression suggested she was trying hard not to smile. "You proposed, you've got to go through with it, or we'll hunt you down and force you up that aisle."

Olympus peeked through his fingers. "Really?"

I shook my head. "No, not really. Stop being mean to him, or he'll run away."

"Can't we be a little mean to him?" Luna said. "We need to make sure he's worthy of you."

"Okay. A tiny bit." I headed to the counter where Albert was waiting to take my order.

I looked back at the gaggle of friends and familiars and my smile almost split my face.

I had an exciting and scary future ahead of me, in a place I loved, with my friends surrounding me, and potentially, an amazing new boyfriend joining the team.

And I had a feeling the adventures would just keep coming.

About Author

K.E. O'Connor (Karen) is a mystery author living in the beautiful British countryside. She loves all things mystery, animals, and cake.

If you want to be part of the Witch Haven crew, practice spells, solve a few murders, spend time with amazing witches and their talking familiars, and get a free book, join her weekly newsletter.

Every Thursday you'll get news on the mysterious happenings in K.E. O'Connor's world.

Sign up today.

Newsletter:
https://BookHip.com/QKGDWJW
Website:
www.keoconnor.com/writing
Facebook:
www.facebook.com/keoconnorauthor

Also By

If you enjoyed

Curses and Corpses

turn the page to read an extract from the next Witch Haven mystery. This book features Luna Brimstone as our main witchy sleuth. This baking witch has some huge secrets that are about to explode, and a few murders to solve!

MUFFINS AND MOONLIGHT

ISBN: 978-1-915378-31-6

Chapter 1

"These cakes taste like boiled socks." Mallory Ling jabbed a finger at the box of half-eaten iced cakes on the counter. "I want a refund."

I ran my critical gaze over the cakes and winced. I'd baked them two nights ago. I'd been tired and not concentrating, longing for my bed and to curl up with a romance novel. The cakes had looked fine when I'd taken them out of the oven, but I'd felt something had been off with them, despite being careful with the magic I'd used.

I should have trusted my instincts and made another batch, but Fandango's was backed up with orders, and there hadn't been time to do anything else. That included making sure my baking magic was topped up, so I didn't produce cakes that tasted like boiled socks.

"Mrs. Ling. Are you sure it was the cakes? You said you had an Indian banquet at your party. Maybe the flavors got mixed up."

"Everyone said they tasted strange. You ruined my special day." Mrs. Ling sniffed.

"Excuse me, where's my caramel latte and slice of pumpkin loaf?" another customer said. "I've been waiting ten minutes."

I waved a hand in the air. "Sorry! I'll get right on that."

"Not until you've dealt with this problem," Mrs. Ling said.

"How about a replacement?" I hurried along the counter where our delicious home-baked treats were laid out for customers to browse.

She followed me, her eyes narrowed. "Did you make any of these?"

I bit my bottom lip. "I did. No one has complained about them tasting strange."

"Actually, this scone is stale." Another customer approached the counter with a plate in his hand. "Can I have a fresh one?"

Mrs. Ling arched her eyebrows. "Give me a refund. I'll have to go elsewhere in the future."

"Don't do that. I'll get everything sorted." I nudged the furry butt of my snoozing familiar, Earl, under the counter with my toe. He shouldn't be in here during opening hours, but no matter how many times I told him, he still snuck under the warming cabinet for a nap.

"Where's your uncle? His baking is always perfect." Mrs. Ling's gaze lifted over my shoulder to the kitchen door.

"Uncle Albert is icing a wedding cake, and I hate disturbing him when he's in the middle of one of his creations. We want nothing to go wrong and spoil the bride's special day."

"Try disturbing him, unless you want more unhappy customers."

I sucked in a breath, aware of the sweat on my forehead as Mrs. Ling continued to complain and draw more attention from the crowded bakery. I always did my best, but baking didn't come naturally to me. Not like Uncle Albert. Anything you imagined, he could create. Fluffy meringues, no problem, feather light chocolate sponge, easy peasy, lemon drizzle bars that tasted like sunlight, done.

Me, on the other hand, everything cake-related I touched risked turning into a sludgy, tasteless mess. Well, it did unless I kept on top of things. And I hadn't been doing that lately.

My gaze lifted to the queue of people waiting to get in. It wasn't even lunchtime, and we were rushed off our feet. I should be pleased, but all I felt was a low level of constant panic and a desire to creep out the back door and run.

My gaze settled on a tall man with his shoulders hunched and a cap pulled down low over his eyes so I couldn't see his face.

I squinted at him. He was watching the bakery, and it wasn't the first time I'd seen him. He'd been here yesterday for about half an hour, standing in the same place. He hadn't moved. I'd considered going over to see if he was lost or needed help, but the next time I'd looked, he'd vanished.

Mrs. Ling slapped her hand on the counter. "Luna! I need my cake problem fixed."

A warm hand settled on my shoulder, and I turned, relief flooding through me as I saw Uncle Albert.

"Is everything okay?" His kind eyes crinkled at the corners as he patted my shoulder.

"Everything's great. I was just fixing a customer's problem."

"You were staring out the window, not interested in helping me," Mrs. Ling said. "Albert, do something about these cakes. Try one. They're terrible."

He looked at the box of cakes and frowned. He picked one up, sniffed it, then poked his tongue out and licked the top. "Did you get these from here?"

"Of course. I placed my order last week. They were for my birthday party. Luna made them, and they're not acceptable."

I scowled at her, not appreciating her loud voice or the fact she'd dropped me in it. "They can't have been that bad. You've taken a bite out of every cake."

"To see if I could find one that was vaguely edible."

I opened my mouth to protest, but Uncle Albert patted my shoulder again. "Let's look at what we've got in stock. You can have another box of cakes, free of charge, a refund, and a free donut every morning for the next month. How does that sound?"

Mrs. Ling finally smiled. "I suppose that's something. It won't make up for spoiling my birthday, though."

"Sorry, Uncle Albert," I whispered.

He winked at me as he led Mrs. Ling back to the tempting dessert counter.

I turned away, grabbed the order for the customer waiting for her caramel latte and pumpkin loaf slice, and then replaced the stale scone. I felt terrible for failing Uncle Albert. I had to make sure my magic stopped failing when I most needed it.

With Uncle Albert's help, we cleared the queue of customers in ten minutes. I sank against the counter and sighed.

He smiled at me. "You're too hard on yourself. You shouldn't take it personally when a customer isn't happy. Some people get out of bed on the wrong side or simply need a reason to moan."

"Those were my cakes. I thought they looked good."

"Did you taste them?"

I shook my head. "Sorry, I was tired. And there's only so much cake you can stomach in one day."

"Luna! You're a Brimstone baker. Desserts are in your blood. You should never tire of cake."

I hid a frown. The trouble was, baking magic didn't flow through my blood. And I'd never admit it, but I wasn't a fan of sweet things. They made my teeth ache.

"You've got this. One small bite at a time. And you can always call on me if you need help." He patted his chunky stomach. "There's always room for a little extra cake."

"I don't like to bother you. And you need your rest."

He chuckled. "I'm a long way from being dead. Although I wouldn't mind an early night.

The wedding cake is proving difficult. It's even challenging my magic."

Uncle Albert's surname was Black, and he came from a family with an excellent reputation for creating amazing desserts. I was a Brimstone, and my auntie married Albert when they were both eighteen, joining two powerful, magical bakery dynasties.

"Once the evening rush is over, you can put your feet up, and I'll deal with the cleanup," I said. "It's the least I can do after upsetting Mrs. Ling."

"She'll get over it. She got a deluxe box of treats and didn't pay a thing." He gave my cheek a quick kiss before heading to the counter where a customer had arrived.

I watched him with no small degree of envy. Uncle Albert was a natural with baking and the customers. And I owed him a lot. He'd taken me in when I was young, and I'd been raised by two loving people.

My auntie was no longer alive. She'd died during an unfortunate dark magic event involving my best friend, Indigo Ash, when she was a teenager. I didn't hold it against Indigo. She hadn't been in control of her magic, but I'd lost a much loved auntie during that dark time.

Uncle Albert had been amazing, though, and I'd never felt unloved or unhappy. He was also so patient with my terrible baking. It was a shame I couldn't pay him back by being better in the bakery and taking pressure off him.

Despite what he said, Uncle Albert was slowing down and wouldn't be able to work full time for much longer.

I did what I could to help, but the baking magic that ran through his veins was like treacle covering a warm apple pie alongside a dollop of delicious vanilla ice cream. His magic thrived in the bakery. Whereas my magic... Well, I wasn't sure where it fit. It wasn't great at making everyone's sweet dream treats come true.

But there was no way I was giving up on Uncle Albert or Fandango's Bakery, so I took each day as it came. After all, you never knew what was around the corner.

It wasn't so long ago that I'd been abducted and dragged into limbo. That had never been on my fun things to-do list. But I'd survived. And I'd survive my wonky baking magic.

The bakery door opened, and I looked up, my smile fading as Englebert Whistletop walked in. He was an attractive older man, and, unfortunately, he was also sort of my sugar daddy, with a difference.

I wasn't all in on the sugar daddy experience. There was no hanky panky between us, not that Englebert didn't do his best to get me in the bedroom. But he'd given me an apartment and looked after me. And, most importantly, he was a magical lifeline. Although I was thinking it was time to give up that lifeline. Englebert and his roving hands were more trouble than they were worth.

You might ask, what did Englebert get in return? Well, he got my amazing company, my skills at dealing with his bunions, and a willing ear and dinner companion when he wanted to talk.

"My dear girl." Englebert reached over the counter and took my hand. "I haven't seen you in days." He kissed the back of my hand with his thin lips.

"Fandango's has been busy, so I haven't had time for fun." I smiled and gently eased my hand out of his grip. "You're looking well."

"And you're looking delightful. You must come to dinner."

"Oh, I wish I could."

"Seven o'clock tonight." He raised a white eyebrow. "I can send the staff away."

"I can't tonight. We're so busy at the moment."

"Then tomorrow."

"You go if you want to," Uncle Albert said. "We're not busy tomorrow night, and I can handle the custom baking orders. We should almost be caught up."

I hesitated. Uncle Albert thought my relationship with Englebert was odd. Most people did, considering he was old enough to be my grandpa, but I couldn't give him up. Not yet. Not until I'd found a replacement.

"You see, your uncle approves," Englebert said.

"I just want Luna to be happy." Uncle Albert's smile was cautious as his gaze flicked to me. "Providing you make her happy, then I have no problems."

"I assure you, I make her very happy." A wicked gleam entered Englebert's eyes.

I had to repress a shudder and look away. I knew what he wanted, but there were lines I never crossed. There'd be no naked fun with my wrinkled sugar daddy. His bunions I could handle, but not his withered pink bits flapping in my face.

I was relieved when the bakery door opened again, providing me with a distraction, and my relief morphed to happiness as my three best friends, Odessa Grimsbane, Storm Winter, and Indigo Ash, walked in.

They strolled to the counter, laughing with each other.

Storm arched a brow as her gaze ran over Englebert. "Are you having a day out from the old folks' home?"

"Storm!" I shouldn't have been surprised by the comment. She hated my relationship with Englebert.

Englebert glared at Storm as a vein bulged in his forehead. "I'll leave you and your friends to gossip. Don't forget, dinner at my place tomorrow night. Wear something pretty. And bring that peppermint scented lotion." He turned and walked out of the bakery.

"Wear something pretty?" Storm sneered at Englebert's back as she flipped her dark hair out of her eyes. "I don't know why you put up with that wrinkled old prune."

"I'm more interested in what you're planning to do with the peppermint lotion." Odessa's large eyes sparkled with amusement. "What bits does he want you to rub? You need to be careful. If you get menthol in the wrong places, it can smart."

I grimaced. "His feet."

"Urgh! You're handling those bony old claws. It must be love if you do that for him," Storm said.

"Be nice," Indigo said. "There are valid reasons they're dating." Her expression suggested she was as puzzled as the others.

"The free apartment," Storm said.

Odessa giggled. "The heaps of cash."

"Or he could have a lovely personality," Indigo said. "One that smells of peppermint after he's had a thorough rub down."

They burst into laughter, and I stood with my hands on my hips, glaring at them and trying not to laugh. They didn't understand. Sacrifices had to be made to keep my magic stable. Dating Englebert was one such sacrifice.

"Seriously, Luna, ditch the old guy," Storm said. "He treats you like some doll to dress up and leer at. You must be bored with him."

"I don't know how many times I have to tell you, we're friends."

Odessa nudged Indigo. "Friends with benefits. You could do better. I mean, I know he's stinking rich, but..."

"But nothing. Englebert's got class, and he is good to me. He helped me when I needed a place to live. I like him. He's interesting." When he wasn't demanding inappropriate kisses after one too many brandies.

Indigo wrinkled her nose and shrugged. Out of the three of them, I was closest to her. When we were kids, we'd always hung out together in the bakery after school.

Odessa sighed. "There are so many eligible men in the village. You should try one."

"Point out these eligible men," Storm said. "I don't see any wandering around."

"They run away when they see you," Indigo said. "You terrify them."

"That's their problem, not mine."

"They're everywhere," Odessa said.

"I don't see you dating these eligible guys," Storm said. "And you scare no one, so they're not hiding from you."

Odessa rearranged the napkins on the counter. "I'm busy with the scarecrows and my pumpkins."

Indigo and Storm exchanged a knowing glance. We knew the reason Odessa didn't date. She'd had what she believed was her one shot at true love, and her heart got shattered.

"Anyway, this isn't about me." Odessa smiled brightly. "This is about making sure our friend doesn't make a terrible dating mistake."

"Englebert isn't a mistake. And I'm considering my options. I have everything under control." I glanced out the bakery window again. I didn't feel in control. And Englebert was getting restless. It wouldn't be long before I'd have to put out for my sugar daddy or kick him to the curb. And I wasn't ready for either of those things.

"Have you got time to stop for an early lunch?" Indigo said.

I shook my head. "I'd love to, but it's been busy all morning, and we haven't had the lunch crowd in yet. Another time?"

A huge, sleek leopard named Monty bounded through the door. His eyes shone with excitement, and his tail twitched as he bounced from table to table, greeting the customers, even though not all of them were happy to be sniffed by a huge leopard familiar.

"Monty!" Olympus Duke strode in. He scowled at the huge cat and clicked his fingers. "Get over here and stop bothering people."

Monty wagged his tail. He was the only cat familiar I'd ever seen do that, and I had experience with cat familiars, having my own incredibly lazy black one.

Monty bounded over to Olympus and leaped up, placing two giant paws on Olympus's shoulders. "Can we get cake? I mean, not that I like cake. I like meat. Do they sell meat-flavored cake?"

Olympus shook Monty loose. "We're not here to get food."

Indigo strolled over and kissed Olympus before ruffling Monty's head fur.

I grinned. They made an adorable couple, and I was happy for Indigo. She'd had a terrible few years, getting tangled up in dark magic and losing her family. She deserved all the joy.

"Are you sure you don't have time to stop for lunch?" Odessa said. "And we were thinking of organizing a night out. All we seem to do is work these days."

"I need help." A woman raced through the door and over to the counter. She slapped down a brochure in front of me. "I have to have this cake. It's for a party. My husband was supposed to place the order, but he forgot. I'm so angry, I should smite him with a hex. Useless warlock."

"Give me a minute," I said to Odessa before turning to the quivering customer.

The woman had a stripe of flour down one cheek and what might be powdered sugar covering her bosoms. "I need an eight layer, multi-colored unicorn cake with magic sparkles, edible glitter, and self-lighting candles. And I need it by the end of the week."

"I ... um ... That's a lot of baking. How about something smaller?"

"No! I was trying to make it, but it was a disaster. The layers were wonky, the icing was gray, and when I tasted it, it was disgusting. Please, you're my only hope. It's for my three-year-old daughter. She'll be devastated if she doesn't get her special cake." A tear trickled down the woman's cheek.

I hated letting anyone down, but an eight-layer cake would take a lot of magic, and mine was drained. I glanced at Uncle Albert, but he was deep in conversation with another customer as they looked through a cake brochure.

This was down to me. "I'm sure we can figure this out."

"I don't mind paying extra for the short notice. But it has to be perfect."

"We can make it happen." So long as I got a huge boost to my baking magic and a decent night of sleep. And the way things were going, I wouldn't have time to do either.

"You're an angel," the woman said. "And how about adding a glitter cascade?"

"I'll grab us some coffee, and we can talk options."

As I made the coffee, I glanced out the window again, and a shudder ran down my spine. The guy who'd been watching the bakery was gone, but someone equally unpleasant had replaced him. He was dressed in the familiar black clothing and wide-brimmed hat of Magic Council employees.

I grimaced and focused on making the coffee. The Magic Council oversaw all aspects of magic regulation, and they were pedants and a pain in the butt.

I looked at Olympus and caught his eye. "Is that a friend of yours?"

He glanced out the window and shook his head. "I didn't bring anyone with me. I'm not working today."

"You're always working," Indigo said, a smile on her face.

I bit my bottom lip as the Magic Council employee glared in the window at me. It was never good news when they came poking around your business, and I had a feeling he wasn't here for a chocolate eclair.

I settled the customer at a table with a mug of coffee and a brochure of our cake designs. "Look through this and pick out elements you want to add to your cake. We'll go from there. I'll be back in a few minutes."

She nodded, eagerly poring through the material.

I grabbed a tray of cake samples and headed outside. I needed to deal with the Magic Council head on and see what they wanted.

"Good morning. Can I tempt you to a free sample? Everything is handmade and fresh today." As I got nearer, the man looked familiar.

He peered at the cakes down a long, thin nose. "Did you make those?"

"Of course."

"Then I won't try them."

I sucked in a breath. "Don't you have a sweet tooth? We sell savory items, too."

"I'm here because we've had a complaint about the tainted food you're selling."

The tray shook as my hand wobbled. "Tainted food? You must be mistaken. Everything we sell here is fresh. We're always careful about storing our ingredients."

"You're not that careful. I'm here to investigate this complaint, and if I find anything amiss, I'm shutting you down."

Muffins and Moonlight is available in e-book and paperback

ISBN: 978-1-915378-31-6

www.ingramcontent.com/pod-product-compliance
Lightning Source LLC
Chambersburg PA
CBHW020748190726

48285CB00006B/1926